In England – Now.

Stories & Observations.

Oh, to be in England

Now that April's there,

And whoever wakes in England

Sees, some morning, unaware,

That the lowest boughs and the brushwood sheaf

Round the elm-tree bole are in tiny leaf,

While the chaffinch sings on the orchard bough

In England - now!

Robert Browning.

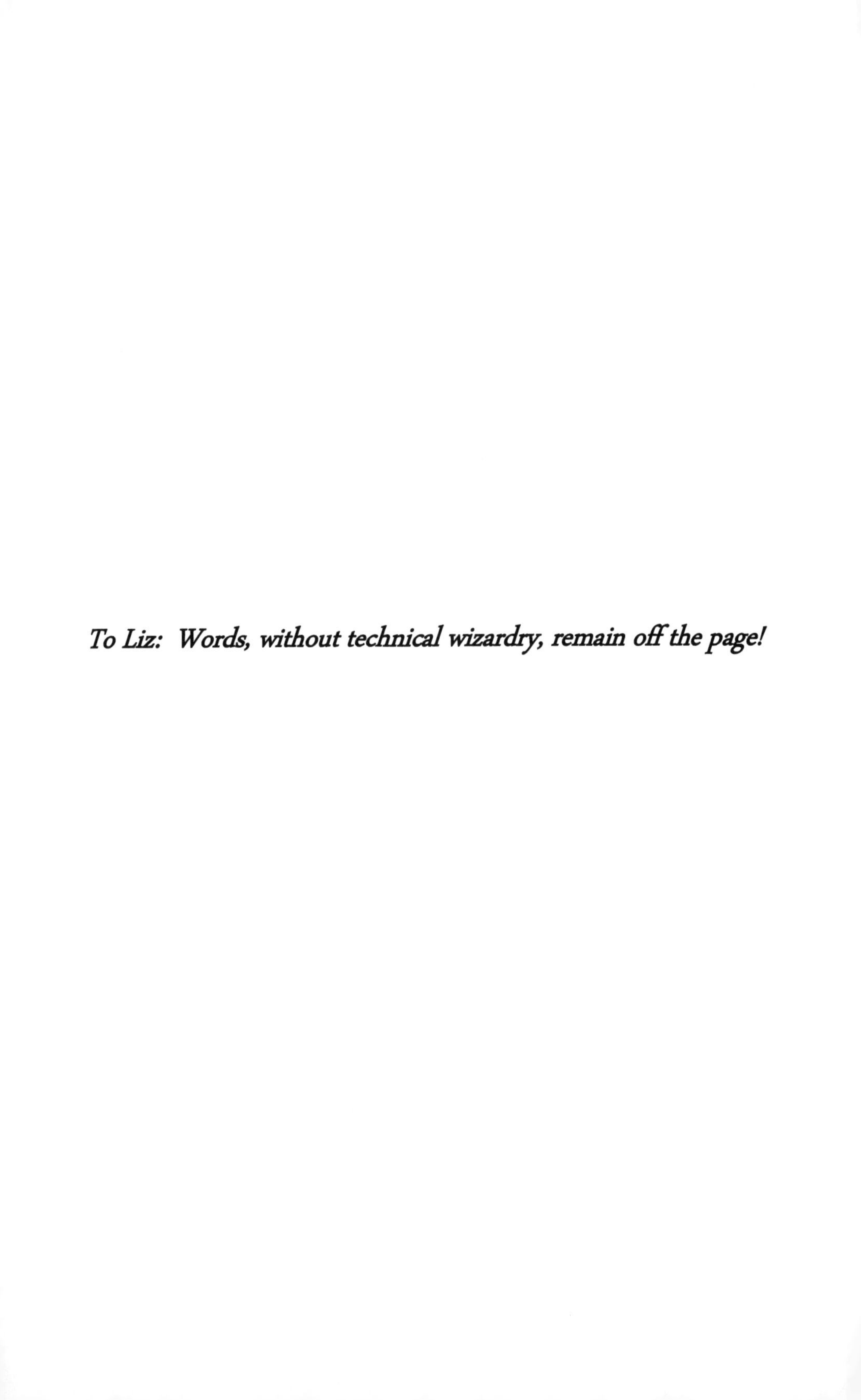

To Liz: Words, without technical wizardry, remain off the page!

Contents

Cold Call

’allo. Elsie Arbuthnott speaking. Two Ts, mind, not just the one.

Oh, yes.

22nd of June, 1930.

Slaughterthwaite.

If I ’ad a pound for each time I’d ’eard that, I’d be a wealthy woman. And do you know, she was as gentle a soul as you’d ever meet. ’Er Mam always used to tell ’er, “Nelly,” she’d say, “dunna fuss about tha’ name, duck; it’s summat and nowt. I always say......”

Oh, yes; sorry. I get side-tracked. Always ’ave done. Me grandma used to reckon .....

Of course; yes. First line of my address. Now, er, yes, uhm. It’s 157b, Avenue Street. ’Ave you ever ’eard owt sillier? ‘Avenue Street’: who on earth thought that one up, I wonder?

Sorry, I missed that; would you repeat?

Oh, I’m not at all sure. Mr. Arbuthnott always dealt with any paperwork. I’ve not really caught-up with stuff since ’is passing. I know I ought to of. I mean, it’s been almost a year, now, but one way or another I’ve let things slip. Envelopes keep dropping on the mat and I put ’em aside, meaning to sit down and sort ’em. But then I find an excuse to put it off, and put it off, and afore I knows it, it's a case of where should I start? So, I don't, and ....

I'm at it again. Very sorry. Now, where was we?

Ah, yes. Well, as I say, I can't really tell you. Anyway, why do you want to know? I should 'ave asked that, first-off. You're not selling owt, duck, are you? "I only buys what I sees with me eyes": that's me grandma again. She'd 'ave no cotta wi' magazines and the like. "You need to see it and feel it, afore tha' puts tha' 'and in tha' pocket." Never wavered, she didn't. Down the market every Thursday she was. Lookin', touchin', even sniffin', wi' fish and meat.

Mortgage? Oh no, duck; no mortgage. Mr. Arbuthnott never liked to borrow. And 'e 'ad good reason, too. Now, an uncle of 'is on his mam's side, Uncle Kenny. 'Kenny Armitage: Carpenter & Funeral Director.' Very skilful with 'is 'ands – and a lovely manner with 'im, 'e 'ad. Anyway or not, ...

Oops. I'm at it again! Can you repeat that? Insurance? No, I don't think so. Council sees to that.

Yes, that's right, duck. Oh, we've always rented. Mr. Arbuthnott was adamant. 'Allo? 'Allo? Are you still there?

Well, really!

Mr. Prufrock Sadly Accepts

{With acknowledgements to T.S. Eliot's *The Love Song of J. Alfred Prufrock.*}

I

Mr. J. Alfred Prufrock is cordially invited to .... .

With a sigh, more hollow than anguished, he pushed the copper-plate printed and embossed invitation aside, and addressed his boiled egg. Like a rather timid woodpecker, he tapped its top, hesitantly inserted the teaspoon's point beneath the now cracked shell, and gently pushed, supporting the egg in its cup with his other hand, and achieving a rather half-hearted beheading. He then used his forefinger and thumb to peel away the remaining shards that still guarded his entry into the breakfast dish he had prepared so diligently. It was a fastidious process, but it was the way he had been taught, at home. Although he was very fond of them, he only ever ate boiled eggs alone; never when breakfasting with others. He felt embarrassed by his timid approach and, absurdly, somewhat envious of those who adopted the more positive method of cleanly slicing-off a boiled egg's top with a knife. He had suffered even greater embarrassment, on one occasion, when invited to remove the cork from a bottle of champagne with a *sabre*. He simply could not bring himself to do it. (Of course, the removing of champagne corks by this, or less flamboyant methods, had certainly not been a skill he would have acquired, at home.)

A second sigh, this one indicating a degree of satisfaction, was released. Gently, he pushed the now empty egg-shell away from him and turned his attention to the remaining slice of toast, which, soon, would be dressed in butter and marmalade. It was a Sunday morning. The only day in the week that afforded him sufficient time to prepare and to eat breakfast. The other mornings saw him swallowing half a mug of tea, anxiously glancing at his watch, and then commencing his "pre-exit-security-routine". Each window latch, each electrical item, each light switch was checked. The words "shut", "locked", and "off" were half-mutedly whispered, as each item passed inspection. Never did he abandon this ritual; never had he found the need for subsequent action; never had he felt sufficiently confident to abandon the purposeless exercise. The remnants of the tea were swallowed. The empty mug was rinsed-out and inverted onto the draining board. The kitchen sink tap was double-checked. Keys were collected from the hook upon which they were always placed, immediately upon his return. Pockets were patted, in order to take a roll-call of wallet, handkerchief, and diary.

Normally, he would be ready to face the day's tasks. But not today. For today was Sunday. *His* day. However, already, it had been disturbed; its purity sullied. He had picked-up the envelope from the carpet onto which it had already tumbled when he had returned, the previous evening. But, anticipating its contents, he had avoided opening it. *Mr. J. Alfred Prufrock is cordially invited to cocktails* ... . Cocktails: his greatest social nightmare (next, that is, to wedding receptions.) The boiled egg, the toast and marmalade, the pot of tea, the sun, streaming through the open window, the prospect of the paper to read, a black-and-white film on TV to watch, perhaps a little doze, ... the untrammelled pleasures of a quiet Sunday, alone, were troubled by that invitation. Of course, he would *have* to accept and, thus, there was no need for internal debate, for pros and cons, for the invention of credible excuses. For he *would* have to go. That knowledge, itself, was sufficient to intrude upon the faux-peace he had embroidered for himself whilst eating his breakfast.

J. Alfred Prufrock .... Of course, he only had himself to blame. That was part of the embarrassment he felt. At home, he had been plain "Jimmy" (although one of his grandfathers had insisted upon calling him "Jim".) When he had decided to re-create himself, he could have settled upon "James", having concluded that the one diminutive was too childish and the other too close to the truth of his roots, which he had spent so much time erasing. Or, rather, allowing others to erase for him. "Alfred" was no invention. "James Alfred Prufrock" was clearly written on his birth certificate. As a boy, he had always done his best to keep his second name secret, fearing that it may be reason to tease, or even to bully him. But, later, life had started to change.

Once "dinner" was no longer eaten at 12.00, which, itself, became "noon", and "tea" became a drink, not an evening meal, so much else had started to change. Coffee was no longer Camp. Barbers became Hairdressers. *Asti Spumante* gave way to *Pinot Noir* and "starters" were translated into "*hors d'oeuvres*". Andy Capp and Garth, two early cartoon cardinal points, were replaced by Giles, at first, and then by Matt. The newspaper Letters' Page offered correspondence somewhat longer than two sentences (lest they were the product of elegant and well-honed wit.) *Amateur Gardener* stood aside for *Country Living*, and *Readers' Digest* was ditched, altogether. Jimmy, to use his mother's phrase, was "getting on". He was poised to make his mark upon the world.

His great-grandfathers had made theirs with a cross; his was to carry a far finer flourish: "J. Alfred Prufrock". It had style. It had gravitas. It had distinction. Or, so he had thought.

Elderly beyond his true age, his watery eyes peered, rather than stared, into the middle distance. His immaculately trimmed, wholly out-of-date, moustache twitched. He brushed a few crumbs from his tweed waistcoat into a linen napkin, which he folded carefully and placed next to his side plate. Why did receptions of any kind cause him such concern? He had attended many in his time. There, he had met some whom he already knew. Or, perhaps it might me more accurate to say, who already knew him. Out of courtesy, they gathered around him and grazed, casually, before moving-on in search of richer forage. He had never accomplished the easy introduction; worse still, he had never mastered the insouciant disconnection. This was the epicentre of his anxiety: how to detach, once he detected the glazed eye of boredom.

Yet again a sigh. This time, one almost signalling decision. He *must* write his letter, accepting the invitation. Then, perhaps, he might return to his poem. It was a form of lyric. A song. He had been working on it for many a Sunday. But, first, he must clear away his breakfast remnants: an empty egg shell; a yolk-encrusted teaspoon; a side-plate, littered with toast crumbs, accompanied by a glistering trace of marmalade, and a smear of butter.

II

Sunday, once more. Once more, the boiled egg and two slices of toast. But an even more anxious repast than the one, three weeks ago, which had ended in his penning a reluctant reply of acceptance to his invitation. *Mr. J. Alfred Prufrock thanks The Chairman & Fellows of the Literati Society for their kind invitation to attend Cocktails and he is delighted to accept.* The theory of proper form, he was entirely cognisant with; it was the more practical aspects of social gatherings that were his torture.

Although he had held-on to the envelope for an unusual length of time before releasing it and allowing it to settle in the post box, he had surprised himself by feeling a degree of relief, once the action was completed. After all, three weeks lay ahead of him; three weeks free from the anxiety of having to pretend to weigh-up a considered decision. It had been taken. His attendance was a fact. The likelihood of any further invitations needing to be addressed during that three-week period was virtually nil. And, who knows, a crisis *could* intervene, resulting in cancellation.

There had been no such intervention. Tomorrow, at 7.30 p.m., cocktails would be served.

Having cleared away his breakfast remnants, he became victim to a sudden invasion of doubts. Cocktails had been but one of the details on his invitation card. In addition to time and place, there had also been *Dress: Black Tie*. So subconsciously determined had he been to erase the forthcoming event from his thoughts during the period of clemency, no attention to attire had been paid. Did he have a freshly-pressed dress shirt? And, if he didn't, whatever was he to do? It was a Sunday; the event was tomorrow!

Of course, one was easily located, neatly folded in a drawer. However, it was not an easy garment, being of the detached-collar and starched-shirt-front variety. Certainly, it would benefit from being unfolded and left to hang. Detached collar; detached collar; where had he placed his detached collar? It was not in his shirt drawer. *Where* might it be? A paralysis of uncertainty left him statuesque in his dressing-room. He could not remember quite how long ago it had been since last he had been required to wear black tie. He had no recollection of where his collars may be located. He blushed. Almost immediately, the blush receded and was replaced by droplets of sweat, teetering on his brow, briefly, and then coursing down his cheeks, in uncomfortably cool rivulets. Then, he quickly thought, there were studs to be found: front and rear collar studs, shirt- front studs. Studs and cuff-links! This, quite clearly, was not destined to be the sort of Sunday he habitually enjoyed.

By midday, that which had seemed to be lost had been found. As had the bow-tie. The dinner suit, first purchased in more youthful years, had been brushed and, where necessary, sponged (oh how he hoped that, once dry, the stains may have vanished!) He had forgotten the hole in his only pair of black socks but, being near the big toe, no one would know, and his patent-leather dress-shoes, once as slick as oil, had only developed the faintest of cracks. He would pass muster, even if unlikely to cut a dash. And, then, the doubts returned. Doubts that would beset him for the next thirty hours, both waking and sleeping.

III

Home from work, as usual, at 5.50, he decided that he must change, immediately. ... *Cocktails at 7.30 p.m.* would require precision-timing. Too early, or on the strike of the half-hour, would demand a time-elapsing walk away from his designated venue. Misfortune may result in his meeting other guests, sauntering together at a leisurely pace designed to bring them to their host's door at just the right time. "Why," they might wonder, "is that strange chap walking in the wrong direction?" Much more than ten minutes beyond the half-hour might suggest incompetence, or ignorance, or ingratitude. And he had not yet finalised the conveyance by which he might arrive. As a walk, it was a longish stretch; it may cause him to arrive, overheated. And, of course, it was summer; it would still be light. Walking the streets, dressed in his finery, and for all to see: it was a prospect that held little appeal to Mr. Prufrock. It also eliminated the bus. Were he to be travelling that distance, ordinarily, he would cycle. Dare he wear cycle clips, dressed in a dinner-suit? Could he summon-up the panache to dismount, de-clip, and attach his bike to a town-house-railings, as his fellow guests arrived? If only it were late- autumn or winter; then, he would be able to fade into the darkness and the folds of his substantial overcoat. But it was still mid-July. A taxi was the safest solution, despite the expense. Yet, even so, he would need to enquire about a precise journey time. "Once more around the block," was not an instruction he was accustomed to giving (nor paying for.) And might not all taxis be booked or taken, at this hour?

IV

"Thank you, so much; I'm most indebted. ... NO! No, this will be absolutely fine. Just a five-minute walk in the air and I'll be nicely to time. Very kind of you." He closed the passenger door, waved farewell to the kindly neighbour, who had seen him leaving his flat, all dressed-up, and had offered him a lift. He stood on the pavement, waving in acknowledgement, still, as the small delivery van executed a neat U-turn in readiness to begin its return journey. Once again, he checked his watch and automatically patted his trouser and jacket pockets before breathing-in deeply and setting-off on foot down a side-street, which took him to a road running parallel to that upon which his host's house was to be found.

His last-minute addition of an umbrella had been a precaution against a steadily darkening sky. The prospect of arriving damp and of spending the first twenty minutes of the party gently steaming himself dry had given him apprehension so strong that it had almost made him breathless. Arriving at the nominated door and having had no need to use his umbrella, it now became an additional impediment to negotiate; nor must he forget it, upon departure. It must be admitted that its seams had become somewhat more frayed than "well used" might normally explain.

It was, as The Speaking Clock would phrase it, 7.39 and forty seconds.

V

As the door is opened, permitting him entrance, J. Alfred Prufrock's heart ceases to flutter and begins to pump. Once over the threshold, he is relieved of his umbrella, which is placed in a stand, already holding several others. He is greeted (not by name but by the more generic yet anonymous, "My dear chap.") The Chairman is in ebullient mood. "D'you know my wife?" and Prufrock is propelled by a gentle but firm pressure in the small of his back towards a tall, graceful lady, who smiles and takes his hand, announcing her own name with unalloyed confidence. Momentarily, she pauses, anticipating reciprocation. When it is unforthcoming, her greeting resumes, flawlessly, as if her tumble of words is gently dropped upon shining ice across which it glides. Her smile never fades and, almost as if she is a pre-programmed automaton, she guides her unresponsive guest towards the drinks table, craving him to select and then to seek-out kindred spirits. She glides back to her husband's side, in readiness for the next arrival. J. Alfred Prufrock is to remain anonymous, both to his host and to his hostess. Had he not troubled to come, they would have been none the wiser.

As he has hoped, his timing has ensured that the party is now sufficiently well-populated for the initial gathering to have divided into smaller groups. Search though he may, he can espy no single individual whom he recognises and to whom he might attach himself. How to inveigle himself into one of these groups of total strangers? He simply does not know. What he does know is that, at a party, a single person, standing alone in the middle of a room, is an embarrassment. An embarrassment to hosts, to other guests, to self. As unobtrusively as possible, he moves towards a wall and feigns interest in a painting, hung thereon. It is the nearest to invisibility that he can manage.

"Are you a fan?" A strongly-voiced interrogative, identical in timbre to that of his hostess. After recovering from his initial startle, he turns, thinking that she has come to his rescue. She, it is not, but another of equal elegance and confident charm. "They have a number, though I'm by no means as convinced as they that he warrants his prices, nor that he'll hold his value, let alone prove to be a wise investment. What's your own view?" Despite how long he has been in front of the painting, he has seen little of it. In his "Jimmy Days", he may well have followed his parents' guide, confessing utter ignorance. But, since then, he has come on.

"I was just trying to place and appraise it," he ventures. He knows the language, even if he rarely speaks it. "I'm unacquainted with the artist, personally, though I suspect a fairly strong Newland School influence," he continues, drawing upon the hours of solitary leafing through books on modern art. It is a subject he has long-felt might be socially helpful.

"Really", his companion responds. He is not sure whether it is a statement or a question. There is a silence. It continues. He knows that he must fill it.

"Not, of course, that I'm any expert. Just the boldness of colour, the brilliance of light. That's the magnet that pulled them all to St. Ives, of course. The light. Its, erm, luminosity. Its radiance. Its clarity. And the sea. Reflections, movement, a sense of vibrancy." That last, modestly developed phrase has been his only successful escape from staccato singularities. How long could he sustain this? How long *must* he sustain it?

"An interesting opinion."

"At last," he thinks, "I've done it; I've actually handed-on the baton for once. This is social exchange!"

"Very interesting, indeed. Now, you really must excuse me; this I simply *must* share with Clemency Bingham-Watts. Do you know Clemency? She'll be fascinated." And, once more, he is alone. Stranded on the edge of some pictorial shore. Maybe in Cornwall; maybe not. He checks his watch. How early may one take one's leave without it being cause for caustic comment? he wonders.

VI

The remainder of the week had been relentless. Even Saturday. Partially through self-will, partially having had little time to give it further thought, the cocktail party had receded far into the darker recesses of his memory. But it had given him cause to think, as he had walked back home through the gloaming, exaggerated by dark clouds and insistent drizzle. How glad he was to have brought his umbrella. It had been handed to him by the factotum at the door. Handed to him without its being requested or identified.

He thought, first, about how the rest of the evening had passed. About the time he had spent treading the margins of the room, feigning insouciance. About his occasional but failed attempts to become a tangent attached to a well-formed circle of conversation. About his sighting of the lady he had earlier encountered; she was speaking to another, quite possibly Clemency Bingham-Watts. As he had looked in their direction, he felt sure that his eye had been caught but when he moved towards them his former interlocutor put her arm around her companion's shoulders and guided her firmly in the direction of another gaggle of chattering ladies. A gaggle that, when thus newly joined, emitted a raucous cloud of giggling laughter. The product of a risqué joke? Of a witty riposte? Of something connected to the Newland School, maybe? Or, ... ? He knew not, and he preferred not to speculate.

And *that* had triggered further thoughts. Thoughts more honest than he ever remembered having had before. Thoughts more attuned to life at home, rather than that of having got on. Thoughts that offered alarming answers to questions he had been asking of himself for many, many years, now.

His return home had found him exhausted and asleep within minutes of settling in his bed. Then had followed five days of non-stop concentration upon his work. But now, at last, it was, once again, Sunday. *His* day.

It was a day upon which he had promised himself two specific tasks to complete: one was the obligatory letter of thanks to The Chairman for a charming cocktail party that had been much enjoyed by all and appreciated, especially, by himself. The other was his poem. That upon which he had been working for many weeks.

He dropped his empty egg shell into his waste-bin, then placed his used breakfast dishes in the hot and soapy water he had prepared for them in his washing-up bowl. He wrote his letter of thanks; inserted it into and addressed an envelope; placed a stamp upon it and put it where he always put letters to be posted the next day. Then he turned to his poem. It was, he reckoned, about four-fifths complete. As it had been, thus far, mostly composed of questions and uncertainties, statements and contradictions, deliberate repetitions, diversions, and hypothetical propositions, "how to finish?" had become a technical problem to wrestle with, Sunday after recent Sunday. Now, at last, he *knew*. The thoughts he had harboured, whilst walking home from the cocktail party, had furnished him with a conclusion as limpid as pure liquor. One so honest and uncluttered, so unalloyed by pretence, so pared-down to common sense that it may not be gainsaid, that it would strike a chord, even with the grandfather who had called him Jim, and everyone else at home.

He found the note-book in which his long-considered, slowly developed, as yet incomplete poem was drafted. Twenty-one lines later, he knew it was finished. He knew it was true. Its theme: his uncontested inconsequentiality.

He put down his pencil, aligning it parallel to the note-book. He re-read what he had written. And, quietly, he allowed two streams of tears to course, gently, down his cheeks. Tears, perhaps, of his self-acceptance; perhaps of modest gratitude for a rare accomplishment completed.

He sighed, hollowly, rather than in anguish. He dried his tears. He allowed his thoughts to move in the direction of supper, for he never ate lunch on a Sunday, given his substantial breakfast. "Perhaps a baked potato," he mused, "or, possibly, cheese-on-toast. I'll ponder upon the options available and decide later." He allowed his limpid eye-lids at first to flutter, then to settle, gently closed, as he drifted into an untroubled doze.

As Per Plan

"Thanks."

"I'm so sorry it has to be in such circumstances."

"No sorrier than me!" Accompanied by the ghost of a self-deprecating, awkward ripple of rueful laughter.

"Of course."

A young man is seated at a table in a coffee shop. An older man has visited the counter to order them each a drink, which he has just carried carefully on a tray and placed upon the table. It's a window table, overlooking a busy street-market, towards which, during his wait, the young man has half-heartedly directed his attention.

The young man's voice is strained and husky; the other's is matter-of-fact in tone, whilst being camembert-unctuous in timbre. A contrasting tension between naïveté and worldly wisdom.

The young man had arrived carrying nothing, whilst his elder companion had tucked a Manilla folder under his arm, as he carried the tray, which he now places on the table, next to his coffee cup. Within the folder are numerous sheets of paper.

That we are witness to some form of personal bereavement seems clear. What, precisely, is its cause eludes us at this particular moment. A silence ensues. A silence during which coffee is sipped, less with relish than with relief. It offers each of them a focus. It fills a void. It prevents an otherwise embarrassing attempt to negate each other's actual presence. However, it is a tactic that cannot be sustained for ever. Clearly, they have come to this coffee shop with a purpose in mind. Whatever that purpose may be.

Is the young man in trouble with the law, perhaps, and the other his solicitor? Certainly, he has the bearing, demeanour, and dress of such. His thick mane of once-black, now-white hair has been styled, not barbered; his Friday-casual suit is of that understated cut that is, itself, a statement. I note the faux simplicity; it must have cost a fortune. Of course, the unarticulated issue may be financial. Tax, insurance, an over-extended mortgage, repossession. Perhaps the older man is an accountant, a financial advisor, an insurance agent, even a bank manager. We simply do not know.

At last, the silent coffee-sipping ritual is interrupted. There is the clink of a cup, placed firmly in its saucer. The scrape of the saucer across the table. The brush of the Manilla folder, and the rustle of the papers within, as they are riffled-through, several times. "Sooo," the older man says, elongating the single syllable. "Let me take you through these documents, for clarification. Feel free to ask about anything you do not understand." The voice reveals a degree of complexity. It does not merely ooze; it is also measured, matured by experience, emollient, but with evident traces of tannin.

"Thanks," comes the cowed response.

"First of all, may I assure you that I, personally, consider you to be a bright, able chap. Bill, of course, *can* be cantankerous. I've had a few set-tos with him, myself, over the years." A chummy chortle. Sympathetic, understanding, soothing words. An unforced confidentiality revealed. "Indeed, he can be brutal. But he's - ," a brief, pensive pause and then, "brilliant! Yes, brilliant, and hugely successful. There's no denying that." A smile follows. Benevolent? Wistful? The papers remain, fanned-out across the open folder, and still not yet referred to.

"I've a few points on my mind that I'd like to clarify," ventures the younger man, hesitantly. He shows no hint of impatience; no sign of insistence; just a mildness born of recognised defeat. Nevertheless, there is the shadow of urgency in his comment.

"Of course," comes the encouraging-sounding reply, rapidly followed by, "Now, the absolutely crucial point is that it should be clear you have *resigned*. All that follows relies upon that." He picks-up the top sheet of paper. "So, here is a letter I've drafted for you; all it lacks is your signature." A neatly composed letter, justified left and right margins, double-spaced lines and paragraphs, occupying a central position on a pristine A4 sheet is passed from the one to the other.

"I've, err. I've written my own."

"You've written your own letter of resignation? Have you delivered it?" An uncharacteristic edge enters the older man's tone.

"Yes." Silence. "I mean, yes I've written my own letter, but no I haven't delivered it. Not yet. I have it with me."

"May I see it? Give it the once-over?" The edge is less sharp.

"Of course." And the young man removes from his jacket pocket another sheet of A4, this one folded into quarters. He passes it over, leaning forward in his chair and retaining that position, looking, anxiously, as his letter is read. Considered. Assessed.

"I would advise against sending this. It certainly won't help your cause; not when future references are requested. Indeed, it may well scupper your chances of picking-up another job within our area of operation. It's all a matter of phraseology, you see, - of indicating that you have a sophisticated understanding of how the system works. *Now*, the one I've drafted for you covers all bases. It's by far the safer version. *Trust me*. You can sign it here, without needing to return to the office. I'll make sure a photocopy reaches you, directly." He plucks an expensive-looking pen, a Mont Blanc, from his inner pocket and places it beside the unsigned letter and then produces a second sheet, saying, "This one merely requires your initials." With an air of apparent disinterest, he adds, "It's of little significance but it just ensures all is as it should be."

"What is it?"

"Oh, just confirmation of what we discussed regarding your intention not to pursue any future legal action against the company. It will hold you in good stead with any potential employer. Now, moving on...."

It is as if the young man recognises that he has swum out of the shallows in which he feels safe and that he has encountered an undercurrent that he knows will drown him unless he grabs for the only fragment of flotsam that may help to keep him afloat. He looks at the pen. But he does not pick it up.

"You mentioned your existing rental arrangements," the older man observes, casually. "Could you run them past me again?" Obediently, the younger man repeats the details of his rental contract: he is to pay his landlord two-thousand pounds per month, over the next three years, with an early-exit penalty of eight-thousand. It had been based upon his belief that his own three-year contract would be honoured in its entirety. A rashness based upon an unexpectedly generous salary offer.

"Gosh, yes!" This, accompanied by a sharp inhalation through clenched teeth. "Well, as I say, you're a bright chap. Disappointment *can* lead to renewed hope, *if* good practice has been demonstrated, previously."

A vacant gaze through the window at the busy market. Banter and barter. Prices shouted; goods purchased. Glossy fruit delicately balanced on a wooden stall. Folk passing to and fro. The quartered sheet of A4 is picked-up and replaced in the jacket pocket. Fingers move towards the pen. They hover. They touch. He signs. The pen and the sheets of paper are returned to the older man. There is no more to do; business has been conducted and concluded.

"Phone me, any time. And the best of luck, young man."

"Thanks for everything," the husky voice responds. They shake hands. Crisply, impersonally. And he walks slowly, with slightly stooping shoulders, towards the door. Then, suddenly, he stops and turns. "Oh, I forgot. How much for the coffee?"

"My treat."

"Thanks. That's kind." And he leaves.

A cell-phone is produced. "Hi, Bill, it's me." Pause. "Oh, a total bloody mess." Pause. "Two grand a month." Pause. "Eight grand to get released from his contract, the poor bastard. Anyway, there you have it. Nothing to be done. I'm on my way back to the office, now." Pause. "Oh, no trouble, there. Pretty straight forward, this time. The one signed and the other initialled. As per plan. Back in about ten." The cell-phone is snapped shut, the papers slotted back into the Manilla folder, a cheery, "Catch you again soon," hailed to the barista, and he leaves, a contented expression suffusing his urbane face.

MELANGE, A LA MODE

“Once upon a time, and not so very long ago, the world was a very much more divided place than it is, today. Now, you may find that very hard to believe but trust me, I know; I was there. Now, I’m not talking about bombs and bullets, Communism and Democracy, North Korea and South Korea. Oh no. I’m talking about a quite different matter, altogether. But we’ll come to that, by and by.”

It was a Saturday morning and on a Saturday morning Mrs. Arbuthnott (“two ts, not just the one, mind you!”) always visited her youngest daughter, who lived but three streets away. She had been mother to four daughters and a son, in her more fertile years. The son had run away to sea when he was fifteen and had been last heard of working for a wildlife foundation of some sort, near Tierra del Fuega. Sexing penguins. “Well,” Mrs. Arbuthnott had declared, upon discovering this, “*somewhere* ’as to be near the Godforsaken place - else it wouldn’t exist at all, would it?” Mrs. A. had a somewhat rhetorical turn of speech and her opinions were never less than rock-solid. Thus, whilst many of her pronouncements appeared to invite discussion and consensus, the inverse, in fact, was always the case. So pleased had she been, on that occasion, with the indisputability of her observation, that she never got as far as commenting upon her wayward son’s occupation. For that, her audience had had a moment’s prayerful silence. Without doubt, Mrs. Arbuthnott’s views on penguin sexing would have been firm, clear, and - how may one best express it? - ‘explosive incandescence’ would not be a description very much wide of the mark.

Happily, judgement upon geographic location, alone, had proved itself to be sufficient. "If the silly beggar wants to live at the arse end of nowhere, then let 'im; isn't that right?" she had pronounced, with a satisfied relish so almost lip-smacking in its intensity that the silence with which it had been met was unnoticed by her.

Having let her son slip through her grip, she made sure that the daughters remained at heel. If determined to marry, they might; but only to men with no ambition to spread their wings. If they chose to remain single, "They've no business wasting money on rent when they've a perfectly comfortable place to rest their 'eads 'ere, where they've been brought-up." Contrary to the statistical norm, all four daughters wed; each of them unusually young. Each was visited by her mother on a fixed day of the week and in order of birth: Monday, Wednesday, Thursday, Friday, and Saturday. Tuesday was Bingo Day, and not to be upset by any paltry need, nor actual crisis. On a Sunday, as had been her habit since first married, herself, Mrs. Arbuthnott cooked a family roast and nothing short of labour-pains or pestilence was permitted to count as an excuse for not attending. Token attempts at rebellion had been made on a few occasions (very few, indeed,) but the resultant fall-out had been such as to discourage any further mad-cap follies. For one daughter to fall short of expectation automatically (rather like Christmas lights, wired in series,) inculcated the others. A wife's misdemeanour was her husband's and, when they started to arrive, her children's, too. To displease on a Sunday was to re-define the meaning of the phrase "a family roast."

And what a roast it always was! Indeed, for the daughters, it always had been, for as long as they could remember. Of her many maxims, Mrs, A. most prided herself on this one: “wasted money on fancy food is no'but financial folly, isn't that right?” Traditionally, a pause – almost Pinteresque in its dramatic impact – fell, here. It allowed her assembled company to recite it, silently, in their minds. The coda was, of course: “And I'm no fool, am I, now?” Within the credo of Mrs. Arbuthnott, food that was fancy was food that was a scruple more expensive than its alternative. And so it was that Sunday roast, *chez Arbuthnott*, was extremely repetitive, both in content and in effect. The second rumen of tripe (“I do 'ave standards as you well-know, now don't you?”) pickled in vinegar and raw onions from Tuesday evening (after returning from the Bingo) to Saturday, come bedtime, whereupon it was placed in cold water to soak until the following morning, before allowing it to simmer in changed water for at least four hours, is both cheap, nutritious, and likely to fend-off the need for very much more to eat, afterwards. Should an appetite be ‘healthy’ (a condition called ‘greed’ by our hostess) ‘seasoned pudding’ would fill the honeycomb holes. Stale breadcrumbs, macerated in and mixed with water, before taking-in a quantity of salt and powdered milk, placed at the top of the oven for three-quarters-of-an-hour, would engender a biscuit closely related to ‘hard-tack’, fondly recalled by all Second World War soldiers, subsequent National Servicemen, and Army Cadets of the 1960s and 70s. Inclined to break teeth and, thus, to reduce consumption, both the original and Mrs Arbuthnott's development, lay in the belly like an unexploded depth-charge. Then came the *piece de resistance*; the centre-piece: the roast, itself. To roast is a process; it's a verb. Its transformation into a noun is a form of grammatical magic. It enhances, and it elevates; it ennobles. It conjures-up images of barons of beef, saddles of lamb, legs and shoulders of pork; it signifies haunches of venison, jugged-hare, spatchcocked-pheasant, cabbage-leaf-protected-partridge. The indulgence of quail. Of grouse. Even a humble chicken, or rabbit. Within the estimation of Mrs. Arbuthnott's value-system, all of this was 'fancy'. Sticking with the process and unmoved by the product, Mrs. Arbuthnott's weekly Sunday roast comprised lights. Heart, stuffed with the seasoned pudding remnants, liver & kidneys (ox, for price-per-weight ratio.) All entered the roasting pan, daubed in lard and simultaneously, from which each item was extracted a about an hour later and left 'to rest', until required for plating-up.

It being Saturday, Mrs. Arbuthnott was visiting her youngest daughter. And chatting with young Marcus, one of her grandchildren. The name had not been accepted entirely with good grace. Indeed, it had been kept a secret from the matriarch until the moment at which any protest she might make was already too late: the baptism, itself. Sitting in the chilly church, Mrs. A. had taken little notice of the proceedings, thus far. "I've been," she always asserted, "to more Christenings than some of you's 'ad 'ot dinners, 'aven't I, now?" Unusually, for her, she tended to leave it at that: an observation that was supposed to fulfil the function of an apothegm. It being an uncharacteristically passive observation, convention was to ignore it. To let is waft, gently, on the breeze of her exhaled breath and to move on. So utterly disinterested in the whole process had she become, following a number of grand-children's baptisms, her youngest daughter had felt it safe to branch-out. How wrong she had been!

"MARCUS?" The reaction was loud, strident, embarrassing. It echoed. "What kind of a name is that?" In fact, the child's intended name was: Marcus, Michael, Maurice - the latter two after his father and his paternal grandfather. The problem was that the Vicar had only proceeded as far as, "I name this child Marcus...............", whereupon Mrs. Arbuthnott had seen fit to shriek. At this precise moment, the infant's nomenclature was *in loco arrestus*! "MARCUS?" The second outcry was no quieter nor no less emphatic than had been the first. "What kind of a name is that, may I ask? We live in Yorkshire, not on't continent; the lad's one of us, not one o' them! Marcus? 'e may as well be bloody Brutus, or, or, or, ..." Other Latinate examples both escaped and further inflated her and it was, perhaps, that sense of inflation which, eventually, procreated what next emerged. "Or bloody Flattulus, for all I know!" It was a magnificent moment. Universal embarrassment gave way to universal laughter. The vicar almost dropped the baby, so seismic was his risible release. Release and relief. Fluently, he intoned,"I name this baby Marcus, Michael, Maurice, ..." And it was done.

Name aside, Marcus became Mrs. Arbuthnott's favourite grandchild. And that is why we find her telling him a story, on one of her Saturday visits. "Oh yes, our Marky; there's something much more than politics and what 'ave you that made us a world more divided than we are now. And shall I tell you what that was?" Of course, it was not a question designed for response, so she proceeded. "It were food; now I'm tellin' you!" She wriggled her backside into the corner of the sofa she had colonised and lassoed her youngest grandchild with an arm that Half-Nelsoned him to her side. "Food; that were what made us different and apart."

"'Ow were that, then, Gran? Grub's grub in't it?"

"Tha's no idea, lad. 'Tis, now, but it weren't, then. British food were for energy, plain and simple. It were like coal into a furnace; fuel into an engine; heat into an air balloon. Didn't taste of owt, but it were 'onest!"

"So what about other countries then, Gran.? What made them so different?"

"Fancy sauces. 'erbs and spices. Garnishes with dressings. And all mixed-up together! 'French cuisine'; 'Indian/Thai/Cantonese/Peking' – all rum forms of sickly cream, rice, and belly-fire, in my opinion, and 'ave you ever known me to be wrong? 'Tex/Mex'; pizza; bloody burgers !" she muttered, as a coda to her castigation.

"But, Gran., why are you so cross about it all?"

"I'll tell, thee, lad: they couldn't keep themselves to themselves. They invaded us. Now *we're* no different from *them*!"

"But isn't that a good thing? Doesn't it make eating more interesting for us?"

"INTERESTING, lad? Interesting? What's interesting about food? It's dead stuff on a plate! I could find more of interest in a bloody cemetery, couldn't I?"

For several further years and on a Sunday, Marcus (along with the rest of the family) endured his gran's family roast lunch. Upon returning home, a supper treat would be Chinese, Malaysian, or Indian take-away. Slowly, he grew-up. Mrs. Arbuthnott passed-on, but he always remembered how his gran. considered cuisine to be *the* great discriminator between nations. At the time, he did not dare to voice his disagreement. Who would have?

But, for him, it's quite different, now. He can state, clearly and without the need either for apology or embarrassment: if we all ate what took our fancy and at the same table, how much better-off we would be. He even discovered a word for such an integrated approach: 'melange'.

"In fact", he thought, one day, "now I'm a writer, wouldn't that be an excellent theme for a short story?"

Trick or Treat

"Would the accused please stand?"

The court usher then turns her attention to the jury, to ask them what verdict they have reached.

It had been a long, twisting path from the start of it all to this point. The friendship that had soured. The apparent opportunities that had foundered. The confident outlook that seemed to have become a confidence trick. And all the loss: loss of trust, loss of truth, loss of integrity. Not to mention loss of money, an attempt at recovering which all this had been generated by.

I had been aware of but not involved with the possibility of a 'project' for over a year. Nothing had materialised. I assumed it to be youthful pipe-dreaming. Though, of course, they had good reason to dream. She, the victim of multiple ill-health that had seen her fail to see the end of her first year at university; he, an ex-young-offender. He had been taken-on, once. Forty-eight hours later, he had been laid-off. An administrative error. An inexperienced junior manager, who should never have employed him, in the first place. Like most others, it was company policy not to employ anyone with a criminal record.

Two young people, both on Benefits; one unsupported by family, the other determined to but not knowing quite how to progress. It had prompted me to write to my M.P., presenting it as but one example of others replicated throughout our towns, cities, villages. Our ‘communities’. The precursor to shop-front sleeping; to, “can you share some change, please?” whispered, pathetically through cracked lips. “I shall forward your letter to the Minister concerned,” came the crisp response. And I waited.

Waiting is no one’s preferred inactivity. We live in a world of instant response. We have become used to pressing a button, which generates an action, which, itself, fulfils our needs. A month of waiting ended with a reminder. I believe the MP had passed the letter on but, of course, had then forgotten it, until reminded. An apology was quickly issued. An assurance that the Minister concerned would be asked to check that the letter had not been over-looked nor mislaid. And, after a while, a response was received. Full of assurances, riddled with hyperbole, concerning Governmental activity, scented with hopes for the future, phrased in that form of professional register that appears to be saying something, but which closer analysis reveals it to be, in fact, flimsier than candyfloss. Mere gossamer. It came from The Ministry of Justice!

A quixotic venture, if ever there were one: nobly intended, naively executed, negative in outcome.

And then, quite suddenly, great excitement! A phone-call. “We’d like to talk with you, urgently; would lunchtime be OK?” The tone surprisingly light, set-free from its usual leadenness.

“Of course.”

“We can’t believe it but it’s really going to happen! See you, later.”

Living on Benefits is by no means as cushy a number as it tends to be presented. Affordable accommodation is not easy to find, nor is it easy to live in. This explains why the Benefits Community tends to be transient. Sometimes, it's the lack of space; sometimes, it's the physical aspects that have self-defined it as 'low rent'; sometimes, it's the neighbourhood. A warring couple, drug-fuelled, violent, smashing-up their own flat and dropping dog-turd outside your own front-door. Threats, prompting Police advice that you might be safer moving out and moving on. Invisible landlords, hiding behind the agencies they employ to peddle their property for them. Freezing (and illegal) temperatures endured in consequence of inadequate heating maintenance. Such are the factors that fail to encourage settlement. Stability.

"We know someone who wants to employ us. You've not met her but she's a business woman who's into horses. She's looking for property to turn into stables and she needs a resident groom and a general handyman. She's got financial backers, and architects, and lawyers, and all-sorts. It's perfect for us."

"That sounds good." A pause, then, "Is there any particular reason you wanted to meet; to tell me?"

"Well, she's offering great rates for individual investors, in addition to the backers she already has, and, obviously, anything that helped to cement our involvement might help speed the process up."

The usual questions about business background, source of major financial backing, experience, and so forth followed. Responses were positive, seemingly well-researched, and enthusiastic. Enthusiasm: that was the key to it. To have seen young people so torpid for so long; dragging their feet around Social Services, and Job Centres; moving from one unsatisfactory accommodation to another - and for over a year, now. Sulks and short-fuses. Rows and reconciliations. Hopes raised, only to be almost immediately dashed. It had been a long time since her eyes had sparkled; since he had registered any degree of enthusiasm about anything. *That* was the temptation. And, if a small profit could be made from it, why not?

Presentations and possibilities, viewings and business plans, on-line searches: the pace increased, and the focus narrowed. An offer was made and accepted. It was going to happen. “We’ll be in by September,” an overly-keen and inexperienced voice asserted, excitedly.

“We’ve been gazumped.” It was a blow. “We’re still the back-up offer and the preferred purchasers, but I can’t possibly manage to stretch beyond this late and extremely competitive offer.” Disappointing though it was, it was nothing out of the ordinary. Disappointment and frustration dominate the world of buying and selling property. The search resumed.

And then the first odd occurrence. The next viable property was being handled by the same estate agency, though from a different office. “Would you mind standing-in for me at the viewing?”

“Why?”

“Well, it’s ridiculous, really, but they won’t deal with me directly.”

"Who won't?"

"The estate agency."

"Why?"

"Not the faintest idea but they won't, so it's a case of someone deputising or of us not being able to take an interest." Enthusiasm overwhelmed inexplicability. Arrangements were made. Discrete questions were asked. Anodyne answers ensued. But the property looked promising. Ill-health was the reason for its sale; and it also explained the recent profit short-falls. The current owner wished to avoid all complications. A quick, fair deal was all he wanted. Nor was he put-off by our revelation that we were acting upon the principal interest's behalf. He had met her and found her very personable. He thought it was a shame that the estate agency was being rather difficult. And difficult though it was being, it was blocking nothing; explaining nothing; content to deal with a proxy.

"I'll be in Italy for a week but you're doing a grand job. Just keep things positive and I'll catch-up with you, next week. Enjoy!" Light, carefree, nonchalant. But rather unexpected. And not a little unnerving. We were by no means expert in this field. We knew that the major backers were carefully calculating potential prospects, but we had (until now,) had no need of further details regarding that aspect. Our job, thus far, had been to nurse the project; to keep it warm; to prevent it from slipping away. But this required a sense of forward movement. Marking time indicates waning interest. This, we could not afford. Progress was essential.

As the point of contact, we started to field certain technical and detailed questions to which we did not have specific answers immediately to hand. Text and email enquiries to Italy failed to generate the data required. We were frustrated. Even slightly cross. But our main motivation remained: to secure purposeful employment for the young pair. We were too close to actualising this to allow personal feelings to squander it.

The next few weeks recorded slow progress and limited release of information. We heard about meetings being held, checks being made, negotiations taking shape. But nothing certain. No hard facts.

"Let me return to the property that was 'gazumped', as you claim. You state that the winning offer was 'late'. As I understand it, by 'late' you mean 'after the closing date'. Is that correct?

"It is."

"Are you absolutely sure about that? Might your memory be mistaken? Might it not merely mean 'later than mine'? Might it not be that you appreciate the different impact between confessing to being 'beaten' and asserting you were 'gazumped'? That, in fact, you invented this unprofessional and immoral act?

"Why should I do that?"

"Vanity, maybe? To gain sympathy? To cover your earlier tracks?"

Silence.

"That was a question!"

"I consider your three suggestions to gain in absurdity, as they progress."

"You had no earlier tracks to cover. Is that your assertion?"

"It is."

"A life of curious, even unique, purity. I congratulate you!" In fact, of incredible purity. Do you understand the word 'incredible'?"

"Yes, of course. It means 'cannot be believed'."

"Indeed, it does! And that is the radial point around which this case orbits: can you be believed? Or, rather, can you be believed? I put it to you that there was no gazumping; that there was, in fact, no later offer at all. 'Later' is only possible in relation to something that has gone before it. The truth is that you never made an offer. You merely claim to have done so. You had led those whom you had gulled as far down this particular path as could be reached. You could see its dead-end. But it was your express intention to open-up further false trails to follow. You needed these folk alongside so that your callous fantasy could be extended."

"Fantasy?"

"Yes. Fantasy. That is what you are: a fantasist. But an imaginary world had ceased to satisfy you, for a fanciful population is as impecunious as are you, yourself. How much richer an experience it would be to import actual, living beings into your fantasy world. And it was. So much so that you needed to bring them so close to the cusp of attaining their own dreams that desperate measures were required to prevent you from

being jettisoned into the reality you had brought them so close to. But into which you had no intention of stepping, yourself." A momentary pause, then, "There is a shorter word for 'fantasist'; one more hurtful in its resonances; a grittier word, by far. That word is, 'liar.' That is what you are: a liar, plain and simple. Is this not so?"

"I deny that accusation, utterly."

"Then we must see what credence or otherwise the jury finds in it. No further questions, m'lud."

A jury's discussions can seem to take an eternity. For the accused, for the barristers, for interested parties, alike. No doubt, for some jury members, too. It is rare for a trial to be straight-forward; an open-and-shut case; hardly worth the time of the twelve citizens, upon whose shoulders, all eventually rests. 'Facts' are capable of interpretation. Defence and prosecuting counsels angle them, and they spin them; they intensify, and they dilute their significance; they assess each jury members' potential outlook, calculating how best to present these facts. Of course, the judge's guidance is invaluable, but it has to be as opaque as ouzo. Only points of law may receive especial emphasis. The two cases presented must, by their lord or ladyships, be rehearsed with a sort of Swiss neutrality. Had counsel for the defence not perceived the possibility of a dismissal, the accused would have been advised to plead guilty and, thus, would receive a lighter sentence. Twelve individuals must discuss, probably debate, certainly exchange opinions for a consensus to be reached. Hours, sometimes days, can be taken over this exercise in justice.

"Have you reached a decision?" the usher asks.

"We have," responds the elected foreman.

"On the count of fraudulence, how do you find?"

As instructed, the other eleven kept their eyes neutrally focussed, as they sat, demurely, in their seats. Their spokesman concentrated upon the usher. The accused, standing as erect as a strongly beating heart permitted, filtered her attention towards the jury benches. It was a tense moment.

Justice had been seen to be done. As the Judge retreated to chambers, stiff formality wilted into a flaccid gathering-together of papers, a shuffling-out of court. A request was made by the prosecuting counsel that his junior should nip-off to prevent those who had brought the case from departing before he had chance for a quick word with them. In a sense, it was over.

And yet, in another sense, it never will be. Not for us. We *know* the truth of it; the Jury had merely done their best to get as close to it as they could. In Law, neatly-tied bows and crisply-starched edges are reserved for stationery and for professional garb, alone. It's different with people. And with outcomes.

Connexions

Now, I bet the Greyhounds amongst you have already sprinted to the conclusion that I can't spell! If you're a Cocker Spaniel, you'll have spotted something out of the ordinary and you'll have decided to lie-down and to observe, whilst awaiting your next instruction. Only if you're an Old English Sheepdog, or an Airedale, even a Westie, will you know there's no big deal, here: you've seen it all before.

"That's an odd way to start," I can hear you saying. And I suppose it is. No odder than the one I encountered at the train station, recently, mind you.

Let me take you into an Upper Crust. It's reasonably early in the day: 9.40ish, or so. My usual flat-white: regular, - large is both too much, and well, too much, if you follow me - is ordered and paid for; now, where shall I sit? No spare spaces outside the bar area, which is also the TV area. Day time TV: a pet-hate of mine. There again, if *I'm* in the right, here, it wouldn't exist at all, having failed every ratings' check known to media-man. But it does; so, demonstrably, I'm wrong. Time to shut-up and to put-up. At least there's somewhere to sit-down and the challenges offered by *Metro* are unlikely to find me defeated by whatever drivel-interference it is that some independent company or another is paying these folk to purvey.

And then, suddenly, he lands with something of a bump! It's a banquette, so the impact made upon it, some fifteen feet away from me (sorry, I'm olde-schoole, come weights and measures,) reverberates and travels, registering in my own rump and, I have no doubt, in those of other punters, further-on down. It is, indeed, quite a belly-flop of landing; but then it would be, considering the size of this particular "bumper": nineteen stones or so of him, by my guesstimation. And, it almost goes without saying, he's ordered the Full English, plus extra slice, to accompany his large cappuccino. The latter he grips in the podgy fingers of his right hand, which constantly conveys container to mouth with robotic regularity.

The awaited plateful arrives. The cappucinno is then put down, freeing his right hand to grasp a fork, whilst the left weilds a knife. Well, perhaps he's left-handed; I don't know. Have you noticed, though, when you're out and about, how many folk, these days, brandish their utensils in what, when I was first taught how to use them, would have been considered to be the "wrong way round"? For once, we can't blame it on America. They, too, favour right-handed forkery, but theirs is a more complex manoeuvre. They start-out as "we used to be"; then, they cut, rest the knife on the side of the plate, transfer fork from left hand to right and eat. I'm trying but struggling to attach this to some aspect of TV Dinner procedure, but I suppose I'll just have to settle for "search me", in pursuit of an explanation.

Anyway, there he is: re-fuelling. (Coming back to Americans, and to portion excess: I wonder if they've got around to coining a word along the lines of 're-calorification', yet? Or am I well-out-of-date on that one, already?)

"Do you have any views on 'The Four Horsemen of the Apocalypse'?"

As a one-line, opening gambit, this is a new one on me. Am I being invited to engage in Biblical exegesis in an Upper Crust at Derby train station? Or is this me barking-up the wrong tree, altogether? Perhaps it's the name of a recently-launched, neo-heavy- metal band that's appeared on "Pop Idol", or some such 'entertainment' programme. My peripheral vision suggests that this is unlikely. Of the various private passions that might float this bloke's boat, rock would appear to be more Scylla and Charybdis than toff-teen-festival-venue. (Yes, I know: more than a little contrived, that jibe, but you must grant that I'm at least making an effort.)

His breakfast (that one, at least,) has been consigned to the historical dustbin of his belly. The coffee has been drained. All that remains to occupy an over- active mouth is conversation. (Perhaps he suffered dummy-deprivation, as a baby. Who knows?) "Did you see it, the other night?" He must be on about something on TV. Could it be a film? I have vague recollections of seeing one, years ago and during my more Art-House days. Not "The Seventh Seal"; chess with the Scythe-toter dominated that, and I'm not sure his three colleagues feature in it, anyway. I *do* suddenly receive this blurred signal from long-since-past: black and white (of course) with all four of them, mounted in a curved dressing (more a phalanx, really.) One of those 'significant' winds that cinema does so well is blowing. Think: an incredibly young Henry Fonda in *The Grapes of Wrath*, or *Scott of the Antarctic*, with Jonnie Mills and James Robertson Justice leaning, heroically, into it, as they strain to pull their sleds. Mind you, if pestilence is about, the last damned thing you want is wind. It may well disipate but, boy, does it distribute! Still, I reckon I'm on to something, here. Or I would be, if only he were to give me a moment or two. But he doesn't. "A documentary about Trump," he added. No doubt feeling the need to drill, remorselessly, into the thickened skull of an ageing yours truly. Wind blowing through the hair of steed-mounted end-of-timers > Donald Trump. As transitions go, there's bathos for you!

Of course, I could just ignore him. It seems more than likely he's used to that, given his proclivity to address total strangers, out-of-the-blue, about the end of human existence. Trouble is: I'm not very good at that. I don't think it's really to do with manners (makyth man, though it was instilled into me at school that they most certainly do.) No, I'm afraid I can't claim that moral high-ground. Of course, I'm not exactly un-loquacious, myself. Given the right circumstances. It's a bit like water and fire is conversation: it draws you towards it. I'm sure that we've all encountered that. And I expect we've all found ourselves a little soggy and slightly singed, in consequence. Let alone bored witless! That poem's last line: "Till human voices wake us, and we drown." He must have known what it was like to be bored witless, old T. S. Eliot. Still, he'd worked in a bank, so he'd probably figured-out strategies to deal with it.

Anyway, moving on. "No. Sorry, I didn't catch it." Feigned re-interest in *Metro*. I'm doing quite well, for me. Of course, I'm fighting-off that enticing temptation for all I'm worth. To lie in my teeth. To make it all up. It's like going for a haircut. No sooner is the protective sheet in place than it starts: "Are you off work, today, then?" It's the one facet of going to the dentist that makes it a more bearable experience than a haircut. Yes, you are asked questions, as the work is undertaken, but no reasonable dental practitioner would anticipate an articulate reply. Hairdressers (I tend not to go to barbers; still a bit too close to the butchery practised by their red-and-white-striped-pole-displaying, leech-applying forebears for my taste) are more expectant. They're also more insistent. Certainly, reticence is regarded by them as a challenge rather than a signal. A citadel to be stormed; not impossible odds from which, wisely, to retreat. So I lie to them. I tell them the first thing that comes into my head. I gee 'em up and I keep 'em going. To the very last snip, and to the would I like any 'product' moment. (Always, I know not why, in the singular: 'product'.) "No, let what's left of it waft in the breeze," I cheerily reply. I suppose it's this that prompted the late Lord, erstwhile Viscount, Hailsham (both previously and subsequently Quentin Hogg, Esq.) to instruct the Parliamentary razor-and-scissors-man, thus: "I would like my hair to be cut short and in silence!" But I'm no Hogg. I'm the fellah who feels it his duty to fill an awkward dinner party silence. No matter with what nonsense. I'll feign an interest in anything – even sports, if nothing else is available, - to oblige. The lies I have told as my locks are clipped! No wonder 'shriven' embraces both the concepts of coiffure and of confession!

So, of course, my having confessed not to having watched the particular documentary referred to fails, entirely, to silence the garrulous super-heavy-weight. Worse: it grants him licence to provide me with a precis. If that's quite the right word. On and bloody on he goes, my glazing-over eyes and surreptitious watch-glancing failing to quell his enthusiasm, one jot. Or to reduce his blather. (What is it about stout men that makes them spit, so?) THEN, it happens! The absolute and screamingly obvious potential nightmare question is posed. In retrospect, I should have seen it coming, a mile off. You probably enjoy sharper foresight than me. In fact, you've probably been wondering why it's taken me so long to reach this crucial point. ('Note to imaginary editor', you've no doubt been registering for about the last two pages, 'too much faff by far, before this narrator mines the nugget we've been begging him to ease from the seam of slack he's been hacking away at from the very start.')

Sorry about that. It had never occurred to me until this very moment. You know where this is heading; have done, all along, I expect. "Please," you are inwardly begging, "let's just get this over and done with, can we?"

I sympathise. Honestly, I do. It's just that I'm a bit slow off my blocks. Always have been. Anyway, as the blessed Magnus never failed to point-out: "I've started, therefore I shall finish." It's taken a while but we've reached, at last, what some like to call this ramble's 'crisis'; its crux; the centrality around which all else rotates.

"If you're bound for Penzance, may I join you? We would then have ample time to thrash this one out." Obese he might be; obtuse he isn't. Apart from being a monumental (in several senses) bore, it turns-out he may be a bloody mind-reader, too. "If I'm bound for Penzance ... Of course, I bloody am! - Or, was. It's unthinkable: God - it'll take us longer to reach than a flight from Heathrow would take to New York!

But I suppose you've figured all this out, by now. A genuine surprise is the story-teller's greatest challenge. How difficult it is to meet it, successfully. Alas.

A form of unwritten contract begins to form itself in the air; if this were a ghost story, we might call it 'ectoplasm'. Paired seats to Penzance appear to be on (or should that be 'in'?) the cards. Faux enthusiasm regarding the interesting hours that lie before us form another variety of lie, on my part.

"Beware," we were proselytised at school, "your sins are bound to find you out." But it will have been worth it (as, so often, it is!) The "Derby, Birmingham (New Street),

Cheltenham Spa, ... arriving in Penzance at .... " departs from platform 4. A side-step, worthy of an international rugby player, finds me boarding a train on platform 5. Any train; any destination; it really doesn't matter! I am hopeful that a bit of ingenuity will, eventually, find me heading towards my chosen destination but, all-importantly, without my newly-acquired appendage. But, then, you know that, already, don't you? You have anticipated the pay-off line from the start, I expect. No matter how 'experimental' I've set-out to make this story, no matter how inventive in both plot and structure, it's all old-hat to you, isn't it? OK. Go on, then. Have your fun; your moment of glory. "Readers Get One Over On Author! Read All About It. Read All About It!"

But was it really *that* bloody obvious? Oh well. Back to the drawing-board, I suppose. Still, just for a moment, there, I thought I might be onto something. Small beer though it was. Never mind; there's always a next time. Another opportunity. Perhaps better to play safer, in future. Stylistically, I mean.

In retrospect, maybe, "After all, I had already missed my intended connexion, *aeons* earlier!" was not as whimsically brilliant an ending as it had seemed at the time. I really cannot decide. Certainly, it seems to me to be not entirely without merit. Not utterly devoid of original spark. Well, flickering glimmer, at least. There's only one thing for it, I suppose. Let's be *really* radical; utterly 21st century. Why don't *you* tell *me*? Now *that* might be a tale worthy the telling!

Caught Short

It's just shy of 2.00 p.m. on the first day of real winter weather. I'm walking through the city centre and the usual posse of strong-cider-drinking homeless are sitting on the shop-step they have occupied all summer. Their faces, shaded by a combination of their life-style, an outside temperature of 2 degrees centigrade, and a biting north wind, are of an unhealthy, liverish purple.

Actually, one of them is not sitting on the step; he is standing on the one immediately next-door, releasing a mighty flow of urine. "Filthy bastard!" a passing teenager, decked-out in the current street-cool gear, spits out with heart-felt venom. "Why don't you use a lav.? Pissing in the street at 2.00 in the afternoon - disgusting!" And, of course, it is. But the young man's criticism implies that his own, predictable, need to pee on the pavement, some hours later and well after dark, as he stumbles post-clubbing-pissed, down the very thoroughfare he has just walked up, may not deserve equal opprobrium. Such is the cant that surrounds our lives!

I, too, initially, thought this to be unacceptable behaviour. But I was prompted to re-consider. The mighty stream, flowing over the shop-step and down the pavement was testament to the man's desperation. "Why don't you use a lav.?" the young man had asked, rhetorically. And the question deserves to be addressed. The offender was yards away from where there had once been Public Lavatories. No longer. They have been removed. Ought he to have popped into a café, or a pub, or the smart new fitness centre, also within yards of where he stood? Absolutely no chance of *him* being directed towards their facilities: just look at him! Should he have wet himself? Are urine-soaked-and-dripping trousers any less disgusting than a pee-drenched pavement? Unacceptable behaviour, yes; but what were this derelict's alternatives?

And, if this is not too much detail, I must draw attention to his stance. Not a drunken, nor flagrant flaunting, but a pathetically demure cowering, as close into the right-angle of the shop corner as he could manage. He, too, was disgusted by his need.

That there is a target for barbs of criticism to be fired at is beyond doubt. What is more doubtful, however, is quite what that target ought to be. A homeless man, caught-short, or the lack of provision for his needs?

In Raiment Adorned

It is a very special evening in the local theatre, which has commissioned the play. It has been written by one of the city's own rising stars. A premier performance. Its central concern is an event from city history. An event now sixty years in the past. Though, is anything ever totally in the past? When a fire is extinguished, the smell still lingers; the memory fails to fade; repairs or replacements create evident differences from their surroundings, prompting the questions, "Why? What happened?" "The past travels with us from afar/And what we have been makes us what we are." There's a great deal of truth in that.

I go to the theatre quite often. Part pleasure, part duty. I review for a magazine. And I've become well acquainted with its audience. Not just individuals recognised from previous visits: the well-into-his-sixties man with a pony-tail; the terribly disabled girl in the high-tech wheel chair; the very, very tubby bloke who always arrives to take his seat seconds before curtain-up and who is always seated mid-row. His physique prevents a squeezing-past folk who are well-settled. They all have to file-out into the aisle, offer him free passage, and then return to their own seats, just as the performance is beginning. He's always apologetic; but his arrangements never alter. Set texts or dramatized versions of novels on the syllabus attract coach-loads of GCSE and A Level students. Musicals and the annual pantomime are a magnet for family groups, sometimes ranging over four generations. It is a well-run and well-supported theatre. It is not, however, an audience that accurately reflects the cosmopolitan demography of the city in which it is to be found. Substantially, that audience is Caucasian.

But not tonight.

Tonight, the usual average crowd has been substantially supplemented. Whole blocks of seats have been reserved, row after row, by a mass-clientele that is normally in evidence only in singletons or pairs. Black ladies, aged in their late sixties or early seventies. Age is not easy to estimate in these soft, creased faces. But, if I'm estimating correctly, they would have been aged between eight and ten in 1958.

1958 is the focal year of the play's action. St. Ann's, an area of the city now converted into a plate glass shopping centre and gentrified conversions from factory floors to lofty apartments atop internal garaging and other service facilities, is the play's location. As children, this is the area to which their "Windrush" parents would have been directed. The area into which they were born, in which they grew-up, to which they were (mostly) destined to remain – until it was knocked-down and cleared, years after the violence which rampaged throughout the area in that late Fifties' summer.

Those lined and leathery faces reflect years of experience. Mostly matriarchs, these ladies, and those (probably few) who never had been mothers, supporters of extended families. Hard workers, with swollen fingers. Carbolic soap and washboards; manual mangles; flat-irons, heated at the fireside. Black-leaded door-steps and outside lavatories; damp, peeling wall-paper; vermin. It's so much more difficult to maintain housing that will soon be condemned by the City Council. To withstand the antipathy of neighbours, reluctant to acknowledge your existence - let alone your right to exist. All funded by low-paid employment. These ladies have lived. They have survived.

It is only upon heading-out of the auditorium at the interval that I realise they are there: three long rows of them; one behind the other. Whilst most others are on the move, heading to the bar, making for the ice-cream sales-point, looking-forward to a stretching of legs, outside, and a cigarette, these ladies show no inclination to move. They are settled, like a gathered congregation in church, content to chat together until the service resumes.

And it suddenly strikes me! There is something distinct about each one of them. Something quite different from the more regular audience they have joined, to see this particular play. Each of them, without exception, is wearing a hat. Not a picture-hat, nor a pill-box; no berets, no garden-party-straw, no gaudy cotton-print. Each hat is of felt: a soft corona, or a neat trilby. The former fixed by a simple pin for security. These are the hats that they wear to church, each Sunday. These hats, their smart dresses, the matching shoes and handbags to accompany have been deliberately adopted.

In 1958 and in this city, the theatre we are gathered in was yet to be built. There was, however, another that had been built in the Music Hall Era. I remember my mother demanding that we dress-up-smart to attend the pantomime, there. It's what people did. No longer –

except these ladies. They are paying respect. Respect to the theatre and respect to the play. After all, it pays respect to their younger selves; to their experiences. It's mutual. It's a form of reverence, as will be their gathering together in church on Sunday, dressed exactly as they are, this evening.

Although the play's purpose is not polemical, it *is* didactic. History's purpose is to keep us aware; to teach us of what, otherwise, we would be ignorant. The ladies need no teaching; they lived through it; they know. Inevitably, the second session picks-up the pace. The seeds of the crisis develop rapidly; the argument intensifies. Characters present increasingly pertinent points. And the ladies, who are not well-versed in the protocol of Theatre but who are familiar with that of their Southern Baptist Church, join-in. "Oh yes," we hear them murmur, at first. "That's right," with greater confidence. "Tell it how it is," resoundingly. Nothing within the script encourages this. Nor are they a claque. It is the way that they have responded to the Gospels since they first accompanied their mothers to Church. It is reverence and it is affirmation. Much more: it is sincerity of response. A rare and beautiful experience. These days.

SOMEHOW, I DOUBT IT

They appeared to be a suitable match. Similar in age, accents betraying the same sort of social background, a shared interest in The Arts.

When he rose from the table to buy their drinks he was slender, tall, slightly stooped. His hair was once sandy, now dusted with grey, and slightly tufty, rather like a baby's. He had dressed "smart casual": a linen jacket with designer elbow-patches, needle-cord trousers, a light cotton shirt with an abstract pattern that echoed the pale green of the jacket. He had made an effort. Unfortunately, his eye for a sharp clothing combo had been less bullseye regarding fit. The jacket was at least a size too small. From its sleeves protruded too much wrist and forearm; it puckered across the shoulders, making it rise so much that its hem stood proud of the natty belt around his trousers. They, themselves, were too short. Large hands and feet, thus overly exposed, appeared to be even larger. Almost clown-like. This disproportionate image emphasised the stoop and his somewhat loping gait, as he immitated a casual stroll to the bar.

Her eyes followed him. Not the doting eyes of a lover. Inquisitive eyes, sharply observant, but suggesting no especial thoughts or feelings. Neutral eyes, registering and assessing.

The voice ordering the drinks was distinct. It had something of a 1950s screen-vicar from central casting about it. Tenor in timbre; slightly flute-like, plummy, and affected. It was shaped by the mildest of stammers. It carried. Perhaps he had been an old-style schoolmaster; maybe he was an actual vicar, who had decided to go open-necked on the grounds that a dog-collar may seem too formal or official. Certainly, the interchange with the barman indicated a degree of naivete, regarding the choices of beer for him and red wine for her. A naivete at odds with the expert conveyance of a pint glass, the wine, and a glass of water. Had he been practising, perhaps?

Certainly, she was impressed. "Bravo! Well done, you," she congratulated him. This was received with a high-pitched "Ha!" If he had been practising, the time taken had clearly been worth it.

That this was their first meeting and that they had been matched by a dating- agency became evident as they settled into conversation. A cross between informal interview and autobiography. The Arts triggered the start of their exchange. A local complex was mentioned by her; she *loved* it and visited frequently. He was aware of it but could not quite recall its name, which she readily supplied. His, "Ah, of course," lacked the conviction of close acquaintance. Indeed, he'd been out of touch, for a while. It had been a period of uncertainty. But he was keen to pick-up the threads. She was just about to book a number of tickets; she liked to be well-organised and to have her plans in place.

The time had come for them to move to the carvery and to select their food.

She was dressed and moved with understated elegance. A trim figure but in no way unnaturally thin. The product of nature, sensible eating, regular, but not gym-based, exercise - gardening, maybe, horse-riding, or social tennis. There was something of the one-time ballerina about her poise and balance, as she moved easily towards the carvery. Her clothes suggested both taste and style: a loose-fitting, cream, cotton blouse with a little neat embroidery around its yoke; a colourful, loosely-pleated skirt, and comfortable-looking, casual, wedge-heeled and strapless sandals. The whole outfit murmured softly, 'far from cheap'. The same was true of her hair-style. It looked to be easily-managed (and, no doubt, it was) but its starting point had been in an expensive salon.

As they stood in the short queue, they didn't talk (possibly thinking of topics to consider during the meal) but as soon as they were settled back at table, he opened proceedings. He elected not to ask a question, inviting her response; nor had there been direct cause for him to begin elaborating on the life-history details the agency must have already asked him to provide; but this was his chosen opening gambit. It was quite a filibuster. Patiently, she allowed him full-flow, neither interrupting him, nor putting him off his stride by interjecting a question, or even a vocalised indication of interest, anxiety, or agreement. It took him through a longish marriage, two daughters (now both grown-up and immersed in their own worlds, so he rarely saw them,) the diagnosis of heart-disease, the long, slow, increasingly unbearable descent into unconsciousness, and the home-death of his late wife. The daughters both being in high-powered jobs in London had only been able to make weekends and, even then, until the very end, they alternated so that each only had to trawl-

up to the Midlands once a fortnight. The unavoidable and extraordinary tediousness of the M1, the North Circular, the need to tip the au-pair extra for child-minding (after-all, a house of sickness is no place for a three-year-old), was an impediment to one, and the other had an extremely sporty partner for whom it was rugby from October to mid-March, then hockey until the cricket season, which led into the late August/early September holiday abroad, and back for pre-match training in the latter half of September. Expectation of at least some support, had been the other's. It had been a tense time. To be honest, he felt massive relief when it was all over. Just for a few weeks. But then the guilt hit. According to what moral code could it possibly have been justified? None, of which he was aware. (Even when considering sensitivities, he maintained strict control over his grammar. That, and the doubts he was possessed of suggested that retired Prep. School teacher was a greater likelihood than vicar.) But time passes by. Wounds heal. Balm to the stricken soul can suddenly be discovered at the most unlikely of times. His balm had been Norwegian. They had met in, of all places, the local post office. She was in the queue, wanting to post a small parcel to her brother, who still lived in Bergen, and she was rather anxious that she would miss that day's delivery, so he, who was ahead of her but only wanting to buy a book of second class stamps and a replacement fibre-tip, stepped aside and invited her to take his place. An unusually excitable but typically open Scandinavian, she thanked him profusely and kissed him on both cheeks. It had seemed the answer to a prayer and it had worked for a while. Or, at least, it had appeared to work. But she had proved to be unsuitable. A drinker. Something to do with being Nordic, apparently. It was a blessing when she eventually beetled back to Bergen. "I'm so pleased that you suggested we meet here; the food's delicious – and piping-hot. You mustn't let yours go cold," his lunch partner gently intervened.

"Gosh, yes," he replied, "what an old rattle bag I've been! I'm most awfully sorry." He applied himself to the as-yet-ignored roast.

"Not at all. I know what it's like: one sets-off with the intention of providing a neat precis and, all-of-a-sudden, one realises one's well into book six of a classical epic!" Like her dress sense and her walk, this was understated, effortless, and tinged with self-deprecating wit. "I just feared for your lunch. Personally, I always think that well-cooked food deserves due respect." She released a well-measured chuckle. It was difficult to decide whether this was natural or designed. No matter which, it enabled her to press his pause button without his noticing. After two or three mouthfuls, he rested his knife and fork, and, with some relish, he concurred with her estimate of the food's quality.

"That phrase, 'rattle bag'," she noted, is one I've always enjoyed. My Nanny always used it to me and my sister, when we were children, and frequently in competition with each other for her attention. " 'What a pair of rattle bags you two are!' she would say. Either that, or, 'You two have as much chatter as a cartload of monkeys!'" She smiled, partially in genuine sentiment, partially to continue her subtle process of smoothing-over her interruption. "I should have asked her who had taught her both expressions, but I never did. She was a

Yorkshire woman with an Irish mother. Perhaps that offers a clue. Especially given the decision of Seamus Heaney and Ted Hughes to call their acclaimed anthology, *The Rattle Bag*. Do you know it?"

He had made excellent progress with his plate of food and had drawn-up alongside her. He may not have been paying her due attention. He may not have heard her clearly. He knew she had asked him a question, but he was not at all sure he had a ready answer. Should he ask her to repeat it? Suddenly, he was gripped by that anxiety we have all experienced at wedding receptions: chatting with strangers whom we find increasingly difficult to hear, as the music overpowers the room. But, here, much more intense an anxiety. None of the wedding reception ploys were available. A neutral smile and an inaudible murmur; the hope that they won't hear your response and, thus, its nonsense doesn't matter; a polite "excuse me", indicating an empty glass and the need to replenish it; the carefree conclusion that one's unlikely ever to meet them again, so nothing really matters. None of these escape routes was available. Especially, considering the very point of this lunch-date, the latter.

He recalled something about a Nanny. About Yorkshire and Ireland. A book and a couple of names. But what was the thread that joined them together and formed the basis of the question he had been asked? A few beads of sweat broke on his brow. He knew that he would have to use his napkin. "Of course, the problem with 'piping-hot' is that it can overly warm one, especially on a lovely day like today." He knew it was limp (rather like his previously starched napkin) but it was the best he could manage. A new direction needed to be taken. It followed a brief but pregnant silence. "So, how long have you been on your own, then?"

"Just over five years. It was always likely to be. My husband was significantly older than me. We enjoyed thirty wonderful years and then, rather like that lovely actor, John Le Mesurier, he just conked-out. Bless him." An affectionate smile suffused her face; it emphasised what kind eyes she had. "Our daughter had married, six months earlier. A delightful Aussie named Gregg, who whisked her off to Brisbane. What you might call 'a double whammy'!" Again, this double-loss was related lightly and without a hint of maudlin self-pity. "Emily (our daughter's name) Skypes me, every week, and, since Ritchie, our grandson, was born, four years ago, she has ensured that he keeps-up with his English granny. I've been out to visit them a few times and I'm always made to feel very welcome. With Emmy secure and what is called the passing of 'a decent period' since Richard's death, I felt it was time to pick-up the pieces and seek a new companion. Knowing the odds, it was a prospect he and I had discussed on several occasions. It was something he felt comfortable with and to which he lent his open support. So, here I am!" Again, the chuckle; this time, almost bordering on a girlish giggle.

Her simple statement had provided time for him to recover his composure and for both of them to have cleared their plates. But he could not think of any appropriate comment to make about her story. So, he reverted to his role as host. "Are you keen on pudding or are you, like me, already stuffed?" Was this still nervous awkwardness or was it gauche? Certainly, it was an unusual approach. Retrospectively, he recognised this. "All school puds, I'm afraid: lemon sponge, spotted dick, bread and butter - each with thick custard."

She absorbed his negative signals and, even though she would have enjoyed any of the three, she demurred. "That roast was both delicious and extremely substantial. Thank you, but I don't want to spoil it, so I'll pass on the pudding. Perhaps just a coffee to round-off the perfect lunch."

"I won't join you in the coffee, if you don't mind, but I'll go and get you one. Any preference?"

"A single espresso would be lovely."

"I'll settle the bill at the same time," he said, and moved to the bar.

Of all coffees, even an iced latte, a single espresso is the quickest dispatched. As soon as her empty cup was replaced into its saucer, he picked-up his napkin. Not, this time, to mop his brow but merely (and quite unnecessarily) to pat his lips. She recognised the code: the meal was over.

"Well that really was a lovely lunch. Thank you so much. I'll just pay a visit to the ladies before hitting the road. It's about an hour's journey." And, having noted her direction, she glided past the carvery.

Upon re-appearing, she began heading back to their table but suddenly stopped. It was unoccupied and had been re-laid. Momentarily, she was uncertain whether or not to linger. A young barman rescued her: "Excuse me, ma'am, your companion is waiting for you in the car park."

“Thank you, so much,” she responded and moved towards the exit sign.

“I didn’t bother with the car,” he explained. “I’m only a couple of hundred yards down the road. Which one’s yours?” She approached a two-seater Mercedes, silver in colour and probably about three or four years old. He paid it no attention, but he did say, “Well, I hope you enjoyed your lunch. Shall we fix another date?” And his hand went to his breast pocket, pulling out his diary.

“Lunch was lovely. Thank you very much. Foolishly, I failed to pop my diary into my bag. I’ve got your number. I’ll call you, mid-week.” She moved towards him. He presented his rather bony right hand, causing his sleeve to ride-up, almost to the elbow. Graciously, she took it.

“Till next time, then,” he said. Rather jauntier, this, than anything that had come before it. And off he set, turning left and heading for home. She settled herself in her car, eased it through the crowded car park, and signalled to turn right. The junction with the main road was only a few yards further on. The healthy-sounding acceleration must have been hers, as she eased her way through the gears.

THE BLEAKNESS OF WINTER

It had been a curiously long summer. Starting early, with a shower-free April, and merging into a warmer-than-usual May. June had, for once, flamed, lending latent heat to both July and August. A hose-pipe ban had been declared and, even in late September, short-sleeves and shorts remained the order of the day. Balmy breezes, originating in Southern Europe, whiffled through October and wafted-in a November, free from chilly rain and breathless fog. Bookies were offering long odds on a White Christmas, come Bonfire Night; longer-still, come the 1st of December.

What a shock it was when, with an immediacy quite alarming, the breezes strengthened into gusty winds, their direction changing from the south to the north-east. Siberia was their origin and little lay in their way to abate them. Dry, at first. And biting. Sharp as a bradawl, they bored into the bones of Saturday shoppers, hurrying from the bus to the shopping centre and finding it necessary to mask their faces with comforting scarves, to breath easily. Then came the snow. Not open flakes of crystalline marvel; not gentle parachutes, nestling, gently on a button-nose, as the competing TV adverts depict. Real snow. Tightly-bound. Propelled by the wind. Stinging to the eyeballs. Cheek-numbing. Less fairy-winged-droplets and more demon-driven ballistae.

That long, seemingly ceaseless, summer had made street-dwellers soft. Well, as soft as their lot could ever be. Nights had been acceptably warm. There had been no need to stamp cold feet and to encourage reluctant blood to reach the skin's surface during the darkest hours of the night. Days had been spent begging, collecting, scavenging, rather than sleeping. It had been a relatively easy time. And on it had gone. On, and on, and on. Until, suddenly, the wind changed direction. Until its caresses became punches; its comforting stirrings, whips lashed with frozen cords.

They were unprepared. Some perished. All presented such pathetic sights on regional TV news programmes that the Government, itself, became unnerved. It called upon local authorities to re-double their efforts to find suitable shelter. A safe pair of political hands received unexpected ministerial promotion: Minister for The Unhoused. The Chancellor was ordered to re-juggle his figures, so that funds (insufficient though they might be) could be raised, enabling the new Ministry to be seen to have taken initiative. A significant number of marginal parliamentary seats might so easily be lost in consequence of this unacceptable face of welfare failure.

Just as the summer had lingered far longer than is normal, so did this spiteful winter extend and outstay its welcome. And, of course, many doorways remained occupied. Help rides a steed named understanding, not a nag called policy. Pushing short-term money at a temporary solution is no solution, at all! What had, initially, propelled these folk onto the streets? Why did some prefer to face discomfort and possible death by remaining in their chosen spot, rather than dossing-down in Church Halls and School Gyms, closed for the Christmas break? These are not simple questions; or, rather, they do not generate either simple or common answers. Their lives are as individualistic as anyone's; their anti-society as complex as its more conventional mirror image.

The snow had started in November. March, surely, would see it stop. It didn't. But, there again, what would follow so long a spell of snow and ice? A thaw! Is to be warmer but wetter an improvement? Absolutely not! Dirty drifts of frozen snow had been piled-up so that the roads and pavements could stay open and safe to use. A few consecutive days above freezing, and, like a suppurating boil, they would begin to seep, slowly releasing their filthy matter, within.

Not to be able to escape the wet: that's the rough-living nightmare. And four months' consolidated snow is not swift to disappear, no matter how warm the weather may have turned. To avoid getting wet, in the first place, is the secret, for heavy materials like matted jumpers, compromised but once-thick-woollen socks, sleeping-bags, will not dry quickly. But, then, how do you retain your space? How much better off are you if you are to be dry but drifting? There is an art (and much craft) to this life-style.

To have survived another winter: there is something of our forebears in that outlook; that measurement of time passing. It has about it something approximating to an achievement. The more spiteful the winter, the greater the achievement; humankind pitting its wits against the elements; one facet of Nature versus another.

The Streets: do they carry the force that propels us? Not The City, nor The Professions, nor Technology, nor

Culture, nor - .... ? On the other hand, are these shivering, whispering ("can you spare some change, please?") desperados the last vestiges of a waning gene-pool?

It's been the longest, most sustained, most temperature-record-breaking summer since such statistics were stored. What, I wonder, does winter hold in store for us (amongst whom 'they' must still be numbered)?

An Offer To A Stranger

I encountered her in the check-out-queue, at the Co-op. There were several people ahead of us. She was a petite woman and her basket, whilst by no means excessively laden, was obviously burdensome to her. Would she like to step in front of me? I asked. It was a genuine offer, tinged neither with sarcasm, nor irritation. A gesture of gallantry, if you will. Certainly, I had never contemplated that it might be of any greater significance than that: an offer to a stranger.

That her response was in a different language from my own took me a little by surprise. Nothing about her had prepared me for this. There she stood: just a little over five-foot tall, silver haired, dressed in the style and manner of other middle-aged women going about an everyday task. Shopping in the Co-op; chatting to one another. But this lady was different: she spoke a language I didn't recognise. And yet I half-discerned what she was saying. "Nyhej, nyhej, nyhej," she seemed to say. Although I didn't recognise the language, I seemed to understand her meaning: "Oh, how very kind of you! But, really, I couldn't possibly jump the queue – not even by one place! I may look to be a frail, old thing and, regrettably, there is more than a hint of truth in that, but I have my standards, you realise. Oh yes, indeed! It's not that I'm ungrateful. On the contrary! Such a kind gesture (and, do you know, so seldom encountered, these days.) Now, when I was a girl, men wore hats and raised them when they passed a lady. Even raised them in different manners, depending upon the degree of acquaintance: with flambouyance to the well-known; with restraint – perhaps no more than a few centimeters - to those recognised, yet lacking further intimacy. But, of course, things were so different, then. A gentler world, altogether. So much slower that it seems to me there were more hours in the day, then. Certainly, more daylight. Pale and cool in the early morning; so warm by noon-time, you could feel it in your bones. And, oh, those summer afternoons: walks down country lanes, dog-roses dancing like butterflies feasting on the nectar of Buddleia flowers, as they – the dog-roses – are brushed by breezes too gentle to dislodge their petals, yet of strength sufficient to stir them. And evenings. Oh, evenings that lasted hour-after-hour-after-hour, the sky aglow and suffused, the scent of cut grass in the air, the sound of birds flitting through the hedgerows. OH, good gracious me! I DO apologise; just for a moment, there, I may have wandered a little; I'm so sorry. Whatever must you think of me?! I know it's a little naughty of me but do you know, I think I will accept your kind offer."

"Nyhej, nyhej, nyhej": it speaks so much more than it says! And, so, she sidled past me, manoeuvring her basket with effort and with awkwardness. Of course, it's obvious *what* it means but *where* does it come from? Delivered with a lilting rhythm, it had something of 'the north' about it, to my ear. There again, mine is not an ear to rely upon! The 'j' was certainly not silent; might it be something like Dutch or Flemish? No, not sufficiently 'back of the throat' and phlegm-ridden for that. Should I be looking towards Scandinavia? Finland, maybe. Finnish (like Hungarian) is littered with consonants, or at least that's what I'm led to believe. But, perhaps I should be considering a language with stronger Latin roots: Romanian, maybe?" And, thus, my thoughts circled around her words, rather like a bird of prey hovering over the area in which it knows its target to lie, hidden for now but, with patience, latent lunch.

In the end, I asked her.

“Where are you from?” I ventured.

Like her own earlier response, my question was stripped of sophistication. Similarly, it released far more complex responses than intended. A degree of panic turned her once-placid expression into a momentary tremor of activity: eyes darting, lips twitching, seismic and involuntary flexions of her face. And then she started looking about her. Not in that vague, ‘maybe if I look elsewhere, this troublesome and interfering stranger will disappear’ sort of way. Her circumspection was much more targeted than that. It had purpose about it. She was, without doubt, checking. Had I accidentally happened upon an illegal immigrant, perhaps? Did she fear that I was ‘out to get her’? Would she abandon her basket and flee?

Then she took me totally by surprise. She inclined her whole body in my direction. She took hold of my shirt sleeve, which she discreetly tugged; she lifted herself up onto her toes, increasing her height. And she whispered. Her words were distinctly formed and enunciated with chisel-edged clarity. But they were whispered, with an intimacy more usually reserved for spies, or for lovers.

“I’m from Russia. I’m Russian.” The R had an elongated, snare-drum-roll to it. It betokened an almost assertive pride. But, suddenly, a small tear began to form in first one and, then, in both eyes. “I’m so sorry,” she whispered, hoarsely. “SO sorry.”

Not ‘niej’ but ‘niet’ - unless she had been using a provincial variant.

But the check-out girl was calling-out, loudly, “Can I help you?”

As she emptied her shopping onto the conveyer-belt, I glanced at the newspaper I had placed on the top of my own basket. Putin Must Pay! its headline shouted.

It was too late for expansion. Once I had checked-out my own purchases and paid for them, she had disappeared, struggling with a greater burden than merely the contents of her carrier bag.

"SUCH, SUCH [STILL CAN BE] THE JOYS"

It is said by some that we live in 'broken Britain'. There is abundant evidence to support that claim. Little girls raped and murdered by confused teenagers of both genders; also, by unhinged adults. Street gangs, including eight-year-olds, who will defend their territory and seek to extend it through any means, including death. Racially generated arson, ram-raiding, cyber-bullying. It happens. It, or its equivalent, happened well over a century ago; William Blake noted it and, thus, saw childhood joy to be past tense, only.

I live in a first floor flat. Its glory is its balcony. I often say that I bought the balcony, with an attached flat. That balcony helps to bring the outdoors in. It releases me, from inside, out. Thus, without being nosey, I am well-acquainted with life-next-door. A Sikh family. A huge house. A substantial area that a Brit would deem "garden" but which this family has made "playground". There is grass but it is not lawn; there are goal mouths, and a trampoline, and swings, and slides, and plenty of hard-standing across which scooters, and tricycles, and peddle-cars, and bikes may be ridden.

I estimate that four generations live within the building. The eldest is a turbaned gentleman of some seventy-plus years. He is slender, serene, and seldom vocal. Though, when he does speak, it is with equally calm authority in either of his two clearly fluent languages. An equally slender, silk and satin adorned lady of similar age, flits in and out of the house, though she seldom lingers outdoors. A number of bearded young men, who have not taken to the turban and whose hair is lengthy but cut, flit in and out. They wear jeans and T shirts. Their spouses retain more traditional dress. Their offspring are between about five and nine; they are at compromise stage: jeans, T shirts, and Top-Knots for the boys; gingham frocks for the girls. Then come the lighter-bearded youths, whose partners are less in evidence, but there are babies in prams and push-chairs.

It should not be ignored that there are servants, too. They brush the main entrance into the house, frequently. They attend to (and, I suppose, slaughter) the hens one can hear clucking, next door. They bring-out linen that needs repairing into the brighter light of sunshine. And they cook. A redolence of cooking is perpetual.

But it is the garden that preoccupies me. The grass is maintained, during the summer, but it is not manicured. There are no borders with fragile delphiniums and lofty foxgloves to batter. It is totally child-focussed. Whether the child be toddler, teenager, or transfer-fee-hopeful. And they play together. Noisily, dramatically, uninhibitedly. Whilst yet others use the swings and slides, the trampoline, the small-vehicle-race-track. Then they all suddenly disappear indoors. To eat together. After which, they re-emerge.

They are not quiet neighbours. But they do not row, nor fight, nor curse each other. Not within my sight nor hearing, anyway. Oh, and the little ones' first language is English. Only later, do they acquire their 'homeland' tongue.

I can't pretend to know it all but I see a good deal. I travel on the bus, I go to the city shopping-centre, I walk through the local parks, I overhear snatched telephone conversations, as I sit in the pub, I watch what is happening in the streets. For the moment, we seem to have almost given-up. "Joy" is a short-term response to a treat, quickly forgotten. It's getting the better of a seemingly intractable parent. It's the "free at last" ticket out, and the "can you sub me twenty?" cadge.

But not next door. There, it's .... What's the best way to put it? It's almost like it used to be. "Such, such were the joys...".

The First 'Last Supper'

It had been yet another perfect day in Paradise. How had they occupied their time? Oh, in much the same way as yesterday. And the day before that. And every day either of them could remember since Eve's creation. Blissfully. Together. Untroubled, unhampered, unchallenged.

As usual, a gently increasing light, accompanied by an equally gentle increase in warmth, had stirred them from sleep. As they had opened their eyes, they had beheld a blissful scene beyond the open structure of their bower. A lilac sky, suffused with shades of coral pink and the subtlest hints of orange. A manicured forest of trees, exhibiting even more shades of green than could an expert Japanese Gardener of our own era. Not just shades but modulations. Some leaves were perfectly formed in serrated ovals, articulated circles, or elegant ellipses, some were glossy with a tracery of lighter-hued veins; others were broad, or elongated, or intricately shaped, as if the product of skilful fret-work; yet further species were coniferous and in infinite variety: Larch-needled, Cedar-tiered, Juniper-clustered.

As they arose, they had paused to scan their panorama. From the vertical, the scene expanded considerably. Lawns, meadows, and wetlands; borders, beds, and arbours; flora, fauna, and fertile fields abundant with benison. And the flowers – oh, the flowers! Their colours; their fragrances; their shapes and sizes and staples and stamens: breathtakingly beautiful. Almost as colourful, delicate, and varied was the bird-life. Tiny Humming-

Birds, their beaks longer than their bodies, flitting, lighter than butterflies, in search of nectar that never failed them. Finches, flashing gold, crimson, violet, and emerald, as they darted gleefully amongst the seed-bearing abundance that left them time and plenty for carolling their miniature motets. Birds with crests and coronets, with brilliant bills and sky-borne skills; with plumage, dense and rich and glossy, yet as delicate as gossamer.

Each morning had offered-up this magnificent vista for as long as either could remember. This, and so much more, was their world. They knew no other. And, thus, this day upon which we focus was as others had been, all the days of their lives together, and it was as all their further days should have been.

They had breakfasted, as usual. They had wandered, as usual. They had snipped a little, re-arranged a little, sat and admired a little, and then, the sky having melted from a cobalt intensity into that water-colour wash to which they had first awoken, they had returned to their bower to sit, to sup, to sleep. As usual.

But there was something amiss. Eve's sleep had started to become disturbed, of late. At first, it had hardly been perceptible; indeed, upon awakening, she was not, herself, convinced that it had happened, at all. But slowly, slowly, the sensation had increased. Eve had discovered herself to be a dreamer. It was a subject she had never discussed with Adam, for she felt quite sure that, had he also experienced such, he would have added it to their list of conversation topics. He hadn't raised the issue, so nor had she. And yet, as the nightly visitations had increased, both in frequency and intensity, she had experienced a desire that became almost too strong to resist. She wanted to tell Adam about her dreams. And why should she not? Why did she falter? What was it about these dreams that caused her to feel something she could not define to herself, let alone to another? We would call it a troubled mind; perhaps, even, guilt. Concepts of which Eve was wholly unconscious.

Another dawn. Another day. Another dusk. Another supper-time. Like all their previous suppers, it was sumptuous. As always, they had mounted the steps that took them into their bower. Adam and Eve paused to admire the table that had been spread for them with delicacies beyond our imagining. The shapes, and hues, and fragrances. Fruits that glistered, as if the dew-mist that had gathered upon them, early in the morning, had remained in place throughout the day, still reflecting the last gentle glimmerings of sunshine, as it reluctantly faded from the evening sky. Salads, crisp even to the sight, let alone to the tongue and to taste. A melange of the mild and the peppery; tastes sharp, clear, succulent and sweet, gathering to a mellow warmth lingered and then gradually faded to leave the palate poised for yet further pleasures. And further pleasures there were a plenty. Tiny sweetmeats, twinkling like precious gems; curds and custards; miniature kickshaws modelled in marzipan; shivering domes and castellated towers of miraculous self-support. Crystalized fruits and creamy nut kernels, placed next to cheeses of infinite variety, all redolent of a rich fecundity. The glassware added further glory to their table. It comprised varieties of intricate filigree, magnified and particularised by the liquids therein contained. Honeyed amber in some, in others a clarity achieved in our own world only by the near-emerald sheen of an iceberg. There were shades of pale straw and of autumnal russet, effervescent cerise, and reds ranging from an impenetrable garnet to translucent scarlet. Each of them seemingly alive in flask or goblet, as they, too, absorbed the still-fading light.

To this feast, as to each previous feast, Adam and Eve sat down. All that day, Eve had been reflective. Not remote, nor withdrawn; not inattentive, nor distant. Just reflective. Upon first noticing this, Adam had concluded that, once again, Eve was overawed by the pleasures of Paradise. That she wanted to absorb its beauty; its perfection. And, thus, whilst he had noticed, he had felt no cause for concern. Their supper began as every supper had before it. With relish, with delight, with appreciation. And thus it continued until towards its conclusion. Conversation between the pair had been as it always was: spontaneous, absorbing, companionable. And then, apropos of nothing that had been said before, Eve suddenly stated: “Tomorrow, I want to explore Paradise alone, Adam.”

This was followed by a sensation new to them both: shocked silence. Different from the silence of shared meditation, or observation, or appreciation. Those are silences of contentment. This was not. This felt awkward. It felt uncomfortable. And it lingered.

The dreams that had been disturbing Eve’s sleep had not been unpleasant. Far from it. Indeed, a growing anticipation of them had made the allure of sleep even more attractive to her. Like our own, Eve’s dream-world differed from that in which she lived-out her days. Its edges were less clearly defined; its time sequences operated outside those within diurnal and nocturnal regulation. They told her stories but stories that, mystifyingly, broke the beginning/middle/end format of those which Adam told her. During her dreams, she both encountered and embraced seeming impossibilities. She travelled distances greater than those that measured the expeditions through Paradise which she and Adam had enjoyed and, whilst most of the terrain through which she passed resembled that with which she had become acquainted, there were certain differences. Well, not differences exactly, more accentuations. Her dream journeys, somehow, contained an element that she could only experience, not explain. We might use the word 'variety', perhaps, or 'surprises'. Words unknown in Paradise. Wherever they had strayed in Eden remained the same as where they had started from. The quintessence of perfect beauty. And, just as everywhere looked the same, so too did she respond to everywhere and to everything with common delight and enthusiasm. Not so in her dreams, where the unknown factor she could only feel applied both to what she saw and how she responded to it. Her everyday responses were predictable; those of her sleeping hours much less so. Some she had had no previous awareness of: slight but by no means unpleasant shivers, sudden variations in her breathing, moments when she felt almost as if she had ceased to exist until she then recovered the steady pulse of normality.

She had not planned to say it. When she had heard her own words, as they tumbled from her mouth, she was as perplexed as Adam. Spontaneity, one must suppose, had not been part of their intended destiny. Eventually, Adam repeated her words but with a different inflexion: "You want to explore Paradise, alone?" he said, not intending a direct question but, rather, merely articulating his own lost comprehension. And, almost inevitably, he then underlined it with, "I don't understand."

No more did she.

Thus, the silence resumed.

"Is there an area you wish to see which I have failed to show you?" Adam's question shattered the long-enduring silence. Stolid, reliable, utterly unexposed to incomprehension, before, Adam's instinct was instantly to amend an unforeseen glitch.

"No," she responded, "you have been, as a guide, as you have been in all other respects: exemplary."

"Then, I don't understand," he repeated. And, truly, he did not.

"Nor do I," was all she could offer in response. Somewhat too quickly (as we would understand it) he grasped at this confession and, the very image of magnanimity, he proffered, "Then let's forget all about it."

"Oh no!" Quite sharp, this. Not crossly sharp; not petulantly sharp; not even obstinately sharp. But sharp with the whetted edge of determination. "No. We, or at least *I*, cannot forget all about it. Tomorrow, I intend to spend the day exploring, alone. It's what my dreams tell me I must do, if...... ." She left the sentence hanging in the balmy air.

" 'If' what?"

"I don't quite know."

"But that makes no sense. It doesn't add-up. It's a hiding to nothing." Adam may have generated a whole host more of such measured clichés had he not been prevented by Eve's next response, which she planted, adroitly, mid-expostulation.

"Quite." Her tone was neither shrill nor combative. It was utterly, perhaps infuriatingly, without edge. It was surrounded by a nimbus of pure innocence. This made it uncontradictable.

They retired to bed.

Upon awakening, the next morning, their supper table had been cleared and fresh viands awaited them. The view from their bower was unchanged. So, too, the weather, the bird-song, the proliferation of floral beauty. Everything was as it always had been.

But Adam breakfasted alone. He had not heard Eve stir, just as dawn was breaking. He had not felt her gentle kiss, lightly pressed upon his forehead. Her smile of love for him. Nor had he seen in her eyes the vibrant glint that, even if he had, he would not have recognised.

She had eaten a light breakfast before skipping down the bower steps. There had been a girlishness in her gait, as she had set-off. And, to all appearances, she had known exactly where she was heading. It had been as if she were being directed.

Adam recalled the days before Eve. As at this breakfast time, he had sat in the bower, alone. At first, he had considered himself blessed. Surrounded by magnificence. Indulged in all respects. The proprietor of perfection. Or, so it had seemed, initially. And yet, dutifully dull as Adam was, he had recognised an impairment in Paradise. Of course, he hadn't complained. He hadn't even felt private discontent. He had merely recognised and accepted. Then, one day, he had been, as he perceived it, rewarded for his patience. The impairment had been corrected. Behold, Eve! Where, he wondered did that leave him, now? Worse-off than ever he had been, for sure. That, he did understand.

And so, as is the way, he brooded. Supper had been but a few hours since. Until its final moments, all had been as it ought to be. Would there be, he wondered, such a supper, ever again? The delights of companionship and of shared foods and wines, the comfort of chat, the discovery of previously untasted delights?

"That's it!" So suddenly had the thought come to him that Adam surprised himself by his vocalisation of it. There had not been one impairment in Paradise. There had been two! And now he must rush to resolve the one remaining. He knew exactly what it was and where he had to go, in order to address it. Urgency had never featured in his compliant lifetime but, suddenly, he recognised that neither Eve nor he was as perfectly formed as he had believed. "Untasted delights"! There had been none, for there were none. None, that is, permissible. Eve's dreams had suggested to her something more than static dissatisfaction. Her dreams had been dynamic, desirable, daring. She had dreamed of LIFE!

Life embraces both stolidity and surprises; the regular and the radical; scripted and impromptu performances. Life can be as daring as it can be dull. It both demands, and it provides. It is rash and emollient, thrust and parry, cabbage and caviar. *This* is what Eve's dreams had told her. And those dreams had suggested where she needed to go and what she needed to do, if she were to realise them. Adam's own epiphany propelled him in pursuit of her.

Of course, as we all know, he arrived too late. The juice was dribbling down her chin; a smoky glaze had misted-over her normally brilliant eyes; a mischievous smile fluttered upon her moistened lips. Close-by, there was a subtle but discernible movement. Adam espied a creature that he had never seen before, as it shimmied away, serpent-style, through the blades of lush undergrowth.

Yes, indeed, Adam had arrived too late. Or had he? A question fit for us to consider, as we settle-down to suppers of our own.

Knock-Knock

The pub's busy. It's a Bank Holiday. No time to look around. Zero-in on a spare space and bag it. Then, order a drink, and settle. There's a wedding reception at one end. And it's been tipping with rain all afternoon. The Bride arrives, protected as best she may be, but she's wet and cold. She heads for The Ladies to repair the damage. Others arrive: feather fanciers limp, legs spattered, ill-fitting suit jackets creased and limp. Suede shoes may look smart in window displays - but not when they're drenched.

Other tables are occupied by families, some of them eating dinner at a bizarre time of the day. By work-mates, enjoying a day-off. By regulars who may be found exactly where they are, at this time, any day of the week. And, behind me, by what I take to be a couple of blokes, enjoying a beer. Although there's only one voice in evidence. It's elderly. It's subject-obsessive. For a good twenty minutes it extolls the virtues of lamb for an Easter Sunday meal. The voice compares the qualities of leg and of shoulder; for a celebratory meal, it dismisses cutlets, out-of-hand. It talks of the need to render fat but to retain a hint of pink in the meat. Occasionally, it upbraids the silent drinking partner. At least he's got family to go to; he ought to be grateful; why is he so miserable, when he has so much support? My bringing-up would not permit me to pivot on my seat and to take-in the physical detail of this pair. And, quite rightly, they would have been irritated (at the very least) to become in-house entertainment for the ignorant and the ill-mannered.

Does he want another drink? No discernible response. “Well, I shall,” and the body of the voice emerges, making its way to the bar. Tall. Smartly turned-out: blue blazer and light-coloured chinos. Nowhere near as old as I had anticipated. He carries his full glass back to his table, positioned behind me. “I don’t know why you wouldn’t have one,” he laments. “It’s a Bank Holiday; it’s Easter. You’ve got that lovely lamb roast to look forward to, tomorrow.” Either silence, or a response too quiet to hear. “Do you know, you really are a miserable bugger! I don’t know why I bother with you.”

The wedding party is now settling down. Hair has been tweaked. Hand-dryers have been re-directed to sort-out uncomfortable damp patches. The Champagne’s arrived, and both glasses and volume are raised.

“Go on, then.” The workmates are risking a later than promised return home.

Young, occasional, unregulated groups relax, indicating that the likelihood is that they’ll order food, later, and skip the intended take-away.

Behind me is the same voice. It’s hardly ever stopped. Sometimes it cajoles; sometimes it encourages; sometimes it merely says, “Think how lucky you are. You should be grateful.”

I had only dropped-in for a quick pint. My glass is drained. Time to go home. I get-up, take my empty glass back to the bar, a ritual courtesy to the staff, and, before I leave, I decide to peek at the table that was behind me.

There is only one person sitting at it.

Unexpected Presents

They had decided upon a retro-Christmas. A radical departure. Previous years had favoured minimalism. Not out of idleness; rather from experience. Too many disappointments. Occasions during which boxes had offered children greater joy than contents; cynical or sulky teenagers had disappeared, angrily, to their own rooms, part-way through the meal; the matriarch, had revisited her annual enquiry concerning the point and cost of it all. Her dislike of the festivity was deeply felt but had never been adequately explained.

The matriarch's final Christmas disfavour was now seasons' past. The teenagers had become twenty-somethings. There were, thus far, no young children to bring disappointment. It was the ideal moment to experiment.

A sensibly sized and priced tree, oozing a resonated scent, was acquired. It had even received a treatment, only recently available, to ensure that its needles remained attached. The best of the ages-old decorations combined tastefully with a few newly-acquired and other skilfully hand-made ones. There was no lop-sided fairy; no tattered, cotton-wool-bearded shepherds; no accidentally flickering trail of lights, likely to blow at any moment soon. All was stylish, attractive, stable.

Team-work in the kitchen had generated a well-moistened, admirably-iced, neatly-decorated cake before the end of October, ready to mature over the following couple of months. Sweet-spiced mince had been marinated and mixed, in anticipation of small pies and an old-fashioned suet pudding. The rare availability of quinces in the local market had been taken advantage of and their gradually intensifying scent had overcome any inexperienced uncertainty about their suitability as a substitute for apple sauce. Crab apples (hard to gather, miniature ones) had been painstakingly plucked from a tree in the garden, rather than leaving this annual produce to the bullfinches, as usual. These tiny berries had been de-stalked, boiled in a sugary solution, and strained through muslin, producing a liquid the colour of coral and with a limpid clarity that had made its sore-nailed manufacturers glow with satisfaction. Raw vegetables had been blanched and pickled, then carefully stored in kilner jars. Little luxuries that would keep had been purchased amongst the weekly shops of October, November, and early December, to avoid their bloom being blemished by a heart-stopping, last-before-Christmas bill. A ham, scalded, skinned, its fat cut into diamonds, then studded with cloves and smothered in treacle and honey, had been gently roasted, whilst an ox-tongue had been braised in water flavoured with bay-leaf and star-anise, ensuring a delicious surrounding jelly, once cooled.

Detailed though the preparations had been, scale had been strictly adhered to. This was to be more Cratchit Christmas Supper, than Fezziwig Ball. And all was absolutely as it ought to be, without any anticipation of last-minute frenzy or fear of failure. Even Nature appeared to have noticed the effort expended. The second half of November had been cold but not damp and fog-clammy. Clear and frost-creating night skies had been the norm. Then, towards the end of the first week of December, a cloud-base had gradually formed. The colour of those clouds and the distinctive tang in the air betokened not rain, but certain snowfall. The forecasters explained that this was not to be blast-driven, cheek-grating shards of Siberian snow, nor those damp-tissue-paper shreds, so near to being liquid that they melt upon contact with ground or flesh. This snow was to be star-shaped crystals. Clearly defined, duvet-soft in texture, pure in colour. What you might call, 'cinema snow'. And it was due to start falling during the evening of December 20th. Such precise forecasting would ensure that roads would be appropriately prepared, and that no one would be caught unawares.

Coconut half-shells, filled with seeded fat and hung in various trees, had attracted a host of small birds into the garden: Tits (Great, Blue, and Long-Tailed,) Wrens and Robins, Finches, Sparrows, and beautifully svelte Nuthatches, their oriental eyes carefully outlined with feathered mascara. Corn and crusts, scattered over the snow-covered lawn, invited ground-feeders to join the feast. Pigeons paced, their wings clasped behind their backs, Duke of Edinburgh style, pecking, self-importantly. Gentler by far, their distant kin, doves, flitted like butterflies, landing briefly to take a decorous mouthful before skittering away. A klaxon call announced the arrival of a cock pheasant, burnished in its winter plumage and magnificent against the neutral backdrop that accentuated its colours. An equally hoarse, though far coarser, screech presaged the arrival of a crow. As it landed, no more than a brief but arrogant glance caused the pigeons to take-flight and to circle before re-landing in an area safely distant from it. Funereal of feather; strident of call; assertive in movement: it strutted, militarily, jabbing indiscriminately at whatever fare was on offer. Without doubt, the Sergeant-Major of this white parade ground.

Indoors, a log-fire blazed. Its warmth and crackle and dancing flames combined to augment the sense of cheer with which the house was suffused. What they had rehearsed was poised for presentation. The dress-rehearsal of Christmas Eve merely confirmed what a success they now had on their hands. The skin peeled away from the cooled salmon neatly and precisely; its flesh, pink and moist, lifted from the skeleton, leaving every bone behind it. Accompanied by a subtly-dressed green salad and a Hollandaise that had combined perfectly, it offered the ideal pre-feast supper.

There had once been a time when Christmas Morning had been something of a challenge. Excited children had demanded that adults must be awake, alert, and enthusiastic whilst it was still dark outside and before a powerful brew had worked its magic on jaded palates and lightly throbbing heads. What bliss that this should be, no longer. A natural awakening, a leisurely bath, a gradual coming to terms with the day over breakfast was anticipated. Then the exchange of secretly chosen, unexpected presents. Perfect!

Careful organisation had ensured there was no need for kitchen frenzy. The bird was already prepared; its weight was known and, thus, its cooking time, the start of which was still a couple of hours away. All that remained were a few fresh vegetables to peel and cut; sauces, savoury and sweet, to make- ready; the pudding to place in a slow steamer, and the table to set. Distributed amongst the gathering forces, these were tasks easily achieved without strain. Firstly, though: the oven must be set to warm-up, ready to receive its gift.

But the oven would not warm-up. Nor would its power indicator light-up.

"Just flick the fuse switch, will you?" she asked, unconcerned.

"It doesn't appear to need flicking; it's set as it should be," he responded.

"That's odd. Let's check the lights." No lights.

No active power indicator for the fridge. Nor the dishwasher, nor the freezer. No working kettle. The numbers on digital clocks were flashing. Land-line phones were dead. So was the TV. Taps released a reserved gush of water, gurgled, choked, and ran dry. "Odd", indeed. And all so suddenly.

The house was not exactly isolated, though it was reasonably remote. And they had always been so self-contained. No regular visits to the nearest pub, some mile or so away. No passing the time of day in the local corner shop. Itself, of course, on this most particular of days, closed, anyway.

"Let's check the internet," he suggested, "the back-up battery on the lap-top will be fully-charged." And, indeed, it should have been. But it wasn't. Cell- phones indicated no more life than land-lines. And then something odder, still. Something utterly inexplicable. "What time is it?" he asked. She looked at her watch. And, then, she looked at him.

"But that's impossible!" She recalled rising at about 8.00. She'd made breakfast at between 8.45 and 9.00, loading their dirty crockery and cutlery into the dishwasher, which had performed a rinse-cycle, as instructed. According to her watch, the time was, now, 9.35; so, too, was it according to his. But 9.35 must have passed ages ago. Of course, she hadn't bothered to check, when she had set its temperature, that the oven was working. She had simply assumed that it would be. Thinking back, she realised that it must have been just after 9.30 that she had done this. It should have taken about twenty-five minutes - she always liked to start with a hot oven, which she would then turn down, once her roast was in place. Thus, now, it must be 10.00/10.15. Certainly *not* 9.35.

"Well, let's wait for the kids to arrive; then we'll sort-out what we're going to do." He was still relaxed, buoyed-up by last night's delicious supper and by the way their plans had, until this moment, fallen so precisely into place.

"Yes. Let's do that." Compliant, though considerably less confident.

"At least the bottles still function!" he chuckled, releasing a cork and charging their glasses. "And thank God for this fire!" They settled into their familiar chairs, sipped, and stared. There was no point in setting about the vegetables, given that there was no way to cook them. She had been looking forward to popping-in-and-out. To chatting, casually, to whichever of her children had seen fit to scrape carrots, or to peel potatoes. She felt that her purpose, like a candle flame, had been snuffed-out. She wasn't sure what to do. So, she sipped, and she stared. So, too, did he. He had finished yesterday's crossword; today, there was no paper. Like her, he was somewhat at sea.

Outside, the snow was now falling quite heavily. The sky had darkened from its earlier steely-grey to an altogether darker hue. Although it must be not far off Noon, the light had faded considerably, more suggestive of tea-time than lunch-time.

"Tell you what," he suddenly said. "Why don't I nip up to the pub and see if others have lost their power. You never know, if all's in order up there, we might even be able to steal some oven-space, when they've finished their service. You'd best hang-on here; the kids wouldn't know where to find us if they arrived and found us both out."

She agreed. She was also surprised to realise that she agreed with misgiving. Quite why, she could not understand. But, without doubt, she did not feel easy with this plan.

As it transpired, she need not have been concerned. He was back within a few minutes. "Bloody car battery's dead, too! Now that *is* weird." As if everything else were not so.

The 'kids' referred to were a daughter and a son, each of whom would be bringing a partner. They were due at 'around noon'. The other member of their gathering was Heinz. Heinz was their ageing and much-loved dog. They had rescued him from a local dog-pound, over a decade ago. He was a variety (or, rather, varieties) of Terrier. Currently, he was luxuriating in front of the blazing fire, toasting his tummy, and releasing the occasional snore. Habitually, Heinz was a contented hound.

Which is why a sudden and prolonged howl, piercing the peace of the morning, caused great surprise. Had he been dreaming? they wondered. Had he allowed himself to get scorched? He roused himself from his full-stretch languor, sat with raised ears and looking towards the French Windows, at which he suddenly launched a devil-may-care charge, hitting the glass with his front paws. Another howl followed, and then persistent barking. This was far from his usual behaviour. The object of his disturbance was the crow. His outburst had scattered all the other birds, but the crow stood firm. And then it advanced, pausing a few yards short of the windows but looking at his opponent directly. Defiantly. His expected shock tactics having failed, Heinz fell silent. But it was not a defeatist silence. And it did not last long. The hair on his neck bristled and a rumbling developed in his throat. This was the sound of innate threat. It was the precursor to what Heinz would do next, given the opportunity: he would leap at the crow, grabbing its throat in his sharp teeth and shaking it furiously until its neck broke. The crow knew this. It also knew that the window protected it. It advanced close enough to stab at the glass with its beak; to simulate piercing the dog's eyes. Heinz was driven demented. So out of control had he become that neither of them dared attempt to pull him away from the window. They feared he may savage their hands. A stroke of brilliance prompted one of them to gently pull the cord that drew the curtains, thereby creating an additional barrier between dog and bird. Sensibly, they allowed Heinz to calm-down; for him to come to them for fuss rather than to impose it upon him. This took some considerable time.

Time enough for them to wonder what had happened to the kids. Surely, by now, they should have arrived. How frustrating it was not to be able to make contact. They sat in front of the fire. They sipped at their glasses. They strained to make staccato conversation. This was *not* what they had so carefully planned. Sensible though they were, frustration was bordering upon fear. He cautiously re-opened the curtains. The crow had retreated to the lawn. It was not feeding; it was watching. Watching the house within which they were now imprisoned. Re-settled in front of the fire though he was, Heinz released a rumble from his throat that indicated that he remained alert.

The light outside was fading. It must be mid-afternoon. The kids had not arrived. The crow was still standing sentinel on the lawn.

He wondered whether he should take a quick walk down the road. Maybe the snow was thicker than they had recognised. Perhaps traffic had been halted. There may have been weather warnings on their non-functioning radio. Reluctantly, she agreed that this made sense. With a heavy heart, she said that he should do this. He was just stepping outside for some time. A fact that made her think, suddenly, of Captain Oates. Fussily, she insisted that he should wrap-up well and put on his boots, as if he were expedition-bound. She was becoming a little unnerved. Heinz was not at ease, either. He roused and shook himself. He made it clear that he was intent upon going-out, too. And then she was alone.

Unless we have reason to take note of it, the speed with which winter gloaming becomes pitch-black is something that escapes us. It did not escape her. She decided it was time to close all the curtains. As she did so. she could not help but register something extremely odd. The crow had not sought-out a roost for the night. It remained where it had been: stood to attention; staring implacably at the house. She could not prevent an almost electric tingle from running down the length of her spine. Nor could she avoid a childhood memory arising. Her mother had never explained what it was about Christmas that she so disliked; she had, however, been more forthcoming on the subject of crows. Usually, she was a fearless woman. But she was terrified of the sinister creatures. Why? Well, about that, she had resorted to her habitual reticence.

He and Heinz had been gone a very long time. It seemed. An extremely long time. It eventually became evident. It was impossible to believe that they would be returning, that night. She piled more logs on the fire. And she sat.

Then the pecking started. Like an insistent pulse, at first. Eventually, like a battering. She knew what it was: the crow was determined to break the glass. But it was super-reinforced-double-glazing. Not even that manic creature could penetrate its toughness. And, following a failed salvo or several, it stopped. Her relief was immeasurable. But the ensuing silence became unnerving. Had this bird decided to call it a day? Had it sought-out a branch in one of the many surrounding trees upon which to settle, curling its head beneath a sheltering wing, and so to sleep? Somehow, she doubted it.

All day long the fire had burned brightly. It had generated both comforting warmth and gentle light. On this most extraordinary of days, it had proved to be more reliable than anything else. Then came the puther. A massive down-draught, billowing thick and acrid smoke into the room. Followed by a screech.

The prospect of the crow forcing its way into her house, down the chimney, damaged upon arrival though it may well be, was too hideous to contemplate. She could think of only one response: she piled yet more wood upon the already fierce flames. This caused her to be engulfed in yet more smoke: thick, choking, eye and throat corrosive. Only upwards, through the chimney's channel, did flames break-through. And the screech became intolerable. Hideous. Unendurable.

By first light, the infrastructure of the house was an almost perfectly preserved skeleton, though charred perpendiculars and horizontals still released wisps of smoke into the hazy dawn. There had been a rapid overnight thaw, leaving the crisp, meringue-folded texture of the previous days' snow stained by grimy runnels. So fierce had been the blaze that brick and plaster had crumbled and disintegrated almost instantly. It was as if the blast had blown itself out within minutes, leaving intact the haunting outline of what once had been a home. The garden was undisturbed. But there were no small birds seeking a first meal from fat-filled coconut halves; neither pigeons, nor pheasants strutted over the lawn, nor did doves perform their nervous acrobatics. There was, however, emitted from somewhere deep within the undergrowth, a hoarse, raw, pained, and yet furious crow-caw.

For him, and for the kids, even for the faithful Heinz, a dismal sight. Should they ever witness it.

"In England – Now"

Two roads, running North/South and East/West, intersect at the crown of a three-sided hill, one side of which ascends from the valley of a major river. They have done so ever since travel and routes began. Nestled into one of the right-angles, thus formed, is a pub. Its external design indicates that it was first constructed in c.1910. On this particular site have sat other inns, taverns, hostelries since at least the era of Domesday. The site is logged in that magnificent, eleventh century data-base. Archaeological investigation would, no doubt, reveal it to have played host to pre-Norman resting places, also.

Stepping over the threshold, we cross the red and black geometric patterns of the late-Victorian/early-Edwardian pub's original tiled flooring. There is a touch of Arts & Crafts about it. It is pleasingly uneven, bearing the imprint of many decades of trampling feet. Heavy-booted travellers, stamping off the outside grime, before they enter. No doubt, it will not be thus for much longer; Health and Safety regulations will demand that it be covered by even-surfaced hardboard, then clothed in industrial-weight carpeting. Already, the ATM stands in the entrance-way, as a declaration of the establishment's modernity. The three TV screens attest to an ambience far different from that offered in earlier eras. Heritage is one matter; historical torpor is another. We live, not in a time-warp, but in an organic society. Yet, to lose all touch with our heritage is to lose a part of ourselves. Of our complex social structure. It is an intricate balance that needs to be achieved; as intricate as any mathematical equation.

Drinks having been acquired, we settle at a table positioned at an angle to the main body of the pub, thus enabling a wide-angled view. Other tables surround us. There are also tall stools positioned against pillar-encircling tops, banquettes, and a raised dais. Like the seating arrangements, the clientele is mixed. Flat caps, trilbies, and beanies jostle with day-glow high-vision vests, top pockets cascading silken handkerchiefs, and hoodies. What we can see is mirrored in what we can hear. Short vowels and staccato consonants pierce through softer, fatter accents, just as pints of mild clink in tintinnabulation with glasses of wine, shots, and vodka-or-tequila-based concoctions, coloured primrose yellow or electric-storm blue.

Two young men share a table near the smokers' exit. One is Asian, but just close your eyes: the accent confirms that you are listening to a locally-nurtured youth. The other may also be 'placed'. Not by his physical features but by the back-of-palate-glottal-stops of Eastern Europe. His English is accurate: no struggling for words, no dislocated constructions; familiar idioms and obscenities lend authenticity to his speech. He is angry. Angry and upset. A sudden dash outside and an equally swift return, as he self-consciously wipes away a tracery of tears, indicate distress. Eastern, like Southern Europeans, are that much more emotionally open than those of us who are more Nordic or Teutonic. To be 'European' is to be part of a historical and cultural inheritance as vast and as varied as the land-mass 'Europe' occupies. Flat-lands and mountain ranges; arctic and sub-tropical temperatures; fertile pastures and arid, flint-strewn outcrops.

Falling, naturally, into the role of therapeutic listener to his emotional friend, the other young man focuses his attention upon him. He nods, sympathetically. "Quite," he says, and, "I hear where you're coming from." Occasionally, he attempts, "Why don't you try ... ?" But it's not a solution his friend seeks. He wants fuel for the furnace of his indignation. Something has gone badly wrong and it's *all* down to *her*! *She* must suffer, as he suffers, now!

Let's leave them to their business. Our intrigue may be intrusive. In a small, self-contained booth sit a Sikh and a man of African origin. Whilst the Sikh embraces the turban and long beard of his culture, he is wearing jeans, trainers, and a tee-shirt. His companion sports two-toned patent leather shoes, sharply-cut trousers, and a shirt/jacket combination that ought to be hideously at-odds yet, somehow, 'it works'. On his head, and rakishly angled, rests a bright scarlet beret. Both are drinking lager and their loud exchange, punctuated by belly-laughter, indicates that they are firm friends and having fun.

Although male-dominated, this is by no means a women-unwelcome zone. Perched on high stools is a trio of teen/twenty-something girls. Their grandmothers would have advised that their skirt length might make chairs-at-table a choice of greater wisdom and propriety. Wisdom and propriety holds no interest for these three. It's Friday night. After they have downed a few bombs, they plan to move on. With luck, having arrived unaccompanied, they will have secured partners before they leave. If not, they'll have fun, anyhow! The timbre of their voices sounds to have been roughened with sandpaper; their volume anticipates that of the club they will eventually end-up in. Zoom-in on their lip-gloss, their false eyelashes and sticky mascara, their carefully highlighted cheekbones, their hair, their jewellery, their fake-tan legs (smooth and shining, as if French polished), their 7" heel-blocks. *All* is a careful contrivance. We live in an age of image. We can airbrush our virtual selves; why not the actuality?

Noted but studiously ignored by the girls, a group of lads has gathered around the bar. Their manner would suggest that this is not their first drink of the evening. In all likelihood, a bottle or two of vodka will have been necked between them. Now, it's pints of lager. Some is slurped; some is spilled, as verbal banter gives way to increased physical jostling. They are on a mission. But there are four of them. It is evident that their campaign will result in some minor victories - not without collateral damage, however. Mates they may be, but, already, an age-old ritual is in play. Three of them will be moving on, accompanied; the one unmatched will have to decide whether to tag along, unneeded and unwanted, to spread his search wider, or to sup himself into pre-unconscious nausea. They know this; we know it, too. Which one will fail to pull? There is something as fearfully fascinating as a game-show about this conundrum. Virtual and actual reality meld, as we observe. As we speculate.

Another table plays host to a group of middle-aged ladies. Some with their husbands, some with friends, some making-up-numbers and looking, already, as if they are realising that a sherry at home, followed by a TV-tray-supper would have held greater appeal. There is much shuffling of bottoms, many side-ways glances, much middle-distance focusing. Then a rearrangement is made. The men-folk visit the bar to split a round between them. Some of the ladies move positions, so as to establish a form of female solidarity. Better to gather together and to natter about nothing-much-in-particular than to sit and sip next to an all-too-familiar silence. As the round reaches the table, the men-folk raise a hollow protest. Secretly, they are relieved, as they settle down together for some serious consideration of tomorrow's team selections.

Of course, no pub can ever be complete without its landlord (or landlady.) Ours is called Steve. Like the most successful of his kind, he is mercurial. He glides, effortlessly, around the crowded room, bestowing bonhomie upon all and sundry. His memory for names is phenomenal. There is something of the chameleon about him: instinctively, he knows whether to exhibit concern after those left at home, to enquire about issues at work, to bait, to bluff, to banter. Here, he has been spectacularly successful in managing to integrate as motley a clientele as may be found in any establishment; in any town. This is multiculturalism in microcosm. Here, race, gender, age, socio-economic numeration count for nothing, nor do they mean anything. Here, folk gather; they find ways to co-exist; they mingle as much as they want to and, equally, they establish the right to keep to themselves, if that is their preference. Only Steve must gel with all. It's his role; his vocation; his source of income. Were he not to exist, like other human necessities, he would need to be invented.

For some, these inn-side cross-roads have acted as no more than a comma, or a semi-colon in the sentences of their lives. For others, they have become a full stop, or a new paragraph. The grammar of our existence is complex and controlling. As is our geography: mountain ranges are walls, and rivers are boundaries. They separate, and they contain. They must be scaled and forded; conquered and crossed. Roads are routes. They direct us, and they pave our way. Cross-roads offer continuation for some, new directions for others; sometimes, they offer arrival. They are both 'on the way' and 'there'. This was Bonnie Prince Charlie's route south, and Mary, Queen of Scots'. Pilgrims trod these paths, seeking Easter shriving. Supporters of the rival roses, red and white, made their way to battle, this way. Turning right, as they reached the crown of the hill and dropping down into the valley, lying eastwards, in order to find a suitable place to camp, came those Roman soldiers whose ultimate destination would be Hadrian's Wall. Some Pilgrims never made it to their chosen shrine: at Coventry, or Lichfield, or even far-distant Walsingham. Some soldiers never reached the battlefield upon which they were due to die: at Wakefield, or Tutbury, or Bosworth. Some legionnaires were too sick to march-on towards Chester or Northumbria. They reached the cross-roads and they stopped. They stayed. They mixed, and they mingled. As generation succeeded generation, other travellers, many of whom had planned to move onwards having rested for the night, went no further on *their* journey, adding to the local mix.

But let's have another survey of the pub on this busy, Friday night. Problems have been aired and shared. Some have been resolved; some have been re-kindled. Issues have been probed, theories have been proven, enlightenment (some of it desired, some of it deplored) has been bestowed upon this person and upon that. Ignorance, also, has been revealed. Contrition has dropped its mask to reveal Contrivance; protested Candour has been outed as specious Calumny. The girls have made their selections. It was clear from the start that they were much more interested in being the seekers, rather than the sought, despite the boys' desperate bravado. The rejected lad lingers, briefly. He waits to see the outline of the bus to town pass by the window, then he checks to see how much money he has left. He sighs, drains his glass, and steps-out into the evening drizzle.

Jagpal, the Sikh, and Clarence, the exotic product of an earlier displacement, sup contentedly and look about them. What do they see? They see: an Asian and an Eastern European in animated exchange. They see workmen, in their grime and sweat, still lingering over their pay-packet-pints. They see elderly ex-Servicemen, open-necked white shirt collars surmounting those of blue serge blazers. They see bingo-winged women, all now resolved to have a good time before returning to what they have come to accept as their allotted role. They see youngsters, freed from the trammels of guilt and secrecy, jettisoned into zero-gravity amorality. They see Steve, the landlord, weaving his way around and amongst this tessellation of a clientele. He extracts girlish giggles from the stout ladies; their stolid-citizen escorts guffaw. The evening is settling into its familiar routine.

This scene is quintessential England. Not the tranquil, rural idyll conjured by Robert Browning's lonely and estranged ex-pat thinker from abroad. That was parched-ground, brow-burned nostalgia. A longing for what had never been and never would be. *This* is the England of history. A hybrid race, hammering-out a way of life. An ever-changing *zeitgeist*.

Jagpal and Clarence have seen much, heard much, done much, in their long lives. *Here* may not have been where their family sagas began and their children, grandchildren, future scions may not remain, but *here* is where *they* are of. Like so many before them, they, or their forebears, were on a journey. They had climbed one incline of the three-sided hill, or they had traversed the plateau stretching westwards, and they had paused for breath. They had found shelter, comfort, and sustenance at an establishment nestled-in to the right-angle thus formed by the cross-roads at the crown of the hill. And they had settled. As others settle, also, here, in England - now.

A MIXED-BAG

You and I might say that she died as she had lived: sadly, and lonely. But, then, she was very little like either you or me. Or like anyone, other than herself.

The unexpected offspring of an unexpected liaison, which lasted for over half a century. So unexpected that the couple who produced her had little in their nature that, these days, we call “parenting skills”. Themselves, victims of a world in which children were to be seen and not heard, neither of them had ever really experienced or embraced the concept of ‘love’. The daughter they produced was the result of duty: the duty of a wife towards her husband, of a man towards God, of a singular achievement bringing merciful relief from further acts of obligation.

And she turned-out to be brilliant. So brilliant that her intellect could not be curtailed, even as an act of mercy. Mathematically brilliant. Today, we might say, “autistic”. An academic married to a raw-boned farm-girl, both attempting to raise a child with ‘special needs’ in an age that was in an embryonic stage of understanding such conditions. How ever did God manage to orchestrate such misery?

And yet God was their one point of triangulation. To the father, Newton’s God; to the mother, the Universal Creator; to the daughter, the ultimate escape. She did not need to suffer breakfast with God; nor any other cripplingly silent meal - except, of course, The Eucharist, at which silence is not painful. God was not in their sitting room, as one corrected exercise books whilst the other darned socks, and the third reflected upon abstract concepts way beyond her peers' grasp. Friends, of course, there were none. Well, one only. He was to be found in church - and in her bedroom, once she had locked the door. He, too, was silent but his was a comforting silence and, rather like a fundamental principal of Physics, both equal and opposite to the home-silence that crippled her. It crippled her creative mind; it crippled her metaphorical heart. But, silent though He may be, God would listen to her; His auto-reflex was not, "Oh, do be quiet" - and, thus, there was always a potential for response to the desperate requests, even when not immediately granted. He was the only one to whom the little girl could speak. He and, of course, His son: a co-sufferer.

If beauty is in the eye of the beholder, so, too, is ugliness. All who encountered her, beheld ugliness. As a child, she was not befriended by others. She had no birthday party invitations. As an adolescent, she did not exist to others, except when she became the butt of their cruel comments. As an undergraduate, she was so terrifyingly brilliant that she repelled even the most liberal interpreters of 'attractiveness'. God was the only one who did not steer clear of her. He may not have been generous in His care and concern, but He was there to be consulted. That, itself, was unique, in her experience. He was her Lover; He was her Lord.

The normal pathways for Oxford Mathematicians who secure a Commendatory First are: Academia, Fast Track Civil Service, National Security, or one aspect or another of Actuarial Science. For one reason or another, none of these was open to her. Actually, for one reason, alone: herself. She lacked any social skills, whatsoever. She would never progress beyond the first interview. And she knew it. Whatever else she may or may not be, she was not stupid. Nor was she self-ignorant. All of which, of course, made it worse. Like Salieri before her, she asked her Creator: "why make me brilliant and yet of so little use?"

Also, like Salieri, she received no answer. God may be the ultimate force but He is a silent one. He never actually spoke to her. Not up to this point in her life, at least.

Research for a higher degree may have offered her a solution. But her parents were poor and grants or sponsorship for her kind of abstract purism did not exist. Someone less devout may have muttered, "Another fine dead-end you've led me into." But, like her branch of Mathematics, her Faith was pure. Uncut with even the merest hint of doubt. Potentially deadly.

So, she returned to her parents. And to the tiny, cramped cottage: delightful, if a picture on a calendar; dreadful if an enforced endurance. For her, the calendar's page was never turned. April echoed August, just as January mirrored June. She was the inverse of a taxidermist's specimen: life imitating death, not death imitating life. Like the moth of Prufrock's imagining, she was "pinned, and wriggling".

Then, suddenly, her silence was interrupted. At last; at long, long, last! He spoke to her. His voice was like crystal: all clarity and dazzling definition. Music to a Mathematician's ear. His advice to her was direct. Of course, she *had* to consider it advice and not a command, for He was her loving Lord, not her liege Lord. Or that was what she thought, at the time.

At first, she was only out during the day and she returned to the family cottage to sleep. She was up in a morning hours before her parents and rarely returned before they had retired to bed. When she thought of them, which was rarely, she almost felt something approaching fondness. But approaching from some considerable distance away. And she had *so many* others to occupy her mind. They needed her *so badly, so urgently*! She did not need to seek them out. Like pigeons to someone holding a bag of seed, they flew to her, fluttering and cooing, strutting and preening, ever-ready to be fed. But what do you feed these particular pigeons? When you have no money, yourself? Nor bread to share? *That*, specifically, had been what she had heard the crystalline voice advise her. As she had long-known, "Man cannot live by bread, alone." She had, within her, sustenance greater by far. She had salvation to hand-out.

Her route and her routine were regular and precise. *They* knew where and when to find her. At first, there had been but few. Gradually, their numbers increased. Happily, she thought, unlike bread, salvation is infinite. She could provide for any number, and should bad weather generate just a tiny gathering, there would be no waste. Salvation's elasticity is miraculous! And its dispensation is addictive.

There came an evening when she did not return to the cottage; nor did she the next evening; nor the next. Her (now very elderly) parents did not notice, at first, and when they finally did, they became alarmed. They sat down to calculate precisely how long it had been since they were last aware of her presence in the cottage. They were shocked. Ashamed. Guilt-ridden. They reported her as a “missing person”. The police visited. Notices were posted in public places.

To discover oneself guilty of gross self-delusion is embarrassing. No, it’s much more than embarrassing: it’s gut-wrenchingly soul-destroying. To admit to having been fooled by others offers a share of responsibility. To have been outwitted, or tricked, or manipulated is to have been the victim of degrees of malice or wickedness. It carries with it a scintilla of having been wronged and, thus, of retained self-respect.

But the discovery of her body held no such comforts for her hapless parents.

Had it been the precise and beautiful voice that had advised her to change her routine, that day, or had it been her own whim? In either case, what had, essentially, prompted it? She had set-out as usual. Carrying two bags, containing scriptures, ready to hand to those who asked her for them, she had closed the cottage door quietly and headed-off up the gently inclining footpath. The sky had been clear all night, so there was sharpness in the air. And a scarce-discernible mist rising from the gardens and hedgerows that she had walked past. A few cattle had been moving languidly, as they grazed contentedly. The dawn chorus had passed a couple of hours ago, so bird life was largely silent and invisible. The early commute had not yet begun. It had been a carbon copy of so many previous days. At its start.

Her congregation was not common to each of her cathedrals. Some attended multiple gatherings but most stuck to just one. They were a mixed-bag: rough-sleepers, buskers, drifters; the unemployed and the unemployable; the bored, the disaffected, those on the cadge; truants and run-aways; refugees. None had much to entertain them. Nothing to offer them respite from ...., well, from themselves, really. And, then, *she* had come amongst them.

"What is 'salvation' ?" It was her opening question. Each day; each location. Sometimes, it triggered a response or two; mostly it didn't. And she didn't mind that; its primary function was rhetorical; it framed and focussed what was to follow. Although she was unaware, herself, that what followed was always the same. What had once been coined spontaneously was now a script. And, therein, lay the joke.

Of course, they didn't want to let on. That would spoil their fun. Discipline was required during her performance; its anticipation and, even more so, its subsequent dissection, once she had moved-on, offered laughter enough. And she had no idea. Not until the day that an inner-voice had prompted her changed routine. Suddenly, *all* was changed. It would never be the same again.

It was not *what* she heard them saying about her, as she neared what would normally have been her third location but, that day, was her first awareness. Insults and verbal cruelty she had long been used to. It was not *that* they were talking about her in such terms. Nor even that *they* were saying the things she could hear. Her life experiences had helped her to develop a tougher skin than most. And she was well aware what folk are like. No, here could not be found the cause of her humiliation, of her shame, of her ire. And she was, indeed, angry. Angrier than she could ever recall having been, even in her teenage years. She was furious, outraged, livid! How could *HE* have been *so deceitful*? How *could* He? The *bastard*!

No one saw her slink away. She was missed by many, as the day progressed. Some even cooperated with the police, who visited her known locations, making enquiries about her disappearance. But these offerings led them nowhere.

It was several weeks later that she became subject to a cliché: an inquisitive little dog sniffed-out her body. It was in an extremely remote location, not easily accessed. The burned-out remnants of a small fire were close-by. Torn and charred shards of paper. Scriptures.

And two empty bags.

ELSIE ARBUTHNOTT'S XMAS LETTER

Mrs. Elsie Arbuthnott ("Two ts, mind, not just the one.") settled onto a dining-room chair, somewhat in the manner of a broody bantam hen returning to cosset a clutch of eggs. Her rump wriggled a little; she picked at the pleats in her skirt, rearranging them for increased comfort; twitched her shoulders a few times, and then fell into a form of transient contemplation. It was time to compose her annual 'Xmas Enclosure', as she liked to call it. Other than shopping lists and a decreasing number of cheques ("well it's all direct debits and Pay-Pal, these days, isn't it? Time was when you needed to practise your signature, ready for adulthood, but like everything else it's all become decimated, or digiterised") she rarely put pen to paper, which is why, when she did, it was essential for her to feel settled and comfortable. Thus, she began.

Dear All,

I've taken my teeth out, in preparation for knocking this on the head at one fell swoop. (Whatever that may mean. I've never known, and at my age there's little point in finding out, cos I'd only forget, straight afterwards.) Anyway, I always feel I can chew the cud better without my plates in, so I've dropped them into a modest glass of port-and-lemon I'm treating myself to, then I'll know where to find them when I'm finished. Oh, and I'm in my stocking feet, too; it may only be mid-December but my chilblains have flared-up, already, and I've got a nasty patch of hard skin rubbing against a seam in one of my plaid slippers – I think that bloody pom-pom must be making a bid to invade. How on earth we used to manage with stays and suspender-belts I simply don't know, but we can at least say good riddance to that little lot.

Right, I'm ready for the off. WHAT a year it's been and no mistaking. I tell you I've been down the civic centre to express my democrating rights more often in the last twelve months than ever I permitted the late Mr. Arbuthnott anywhere near me on an annual basis. It's as if you've only just got home for a brew when the mini-bus driver's rattling your letter box wanting to know if you need help buttoning your coat up for the next session's outing. I said to them the last time,"one more how d'you do like this again before Christmas and I'll volunteer to play turkey, myself, and willingly, come the day." Of course, I got no response. They're all the same, these civic servants: po-faced streaks o' nothing what's only interest is the first line of your address.

Anyway or not, "Christmas". Don't go letting me wander-off and following balloons. I have enough-on remembering whether it's breakfast time (two bags of tea and a slice of lightly-browned toast) or mid-morning (one level teaspoon of instant coffee and an arrowroot biscuit) as it is. Not to mention the tablets! 'Now, Mrs. Arbuthnott,' the doctor told me last time, 'it's very important that you remember to take these new tablets in- between the old ones and not at the same time.' It was only that last bit that made me realise he wasn't asking me to make-up a sandwich. I looked him straight in the eye and (very calmly) pointed out that with the yellow ones immediately before eating, the blue ones half-an-hour after eating, the pink ones during a meal, and the white ones on an empty stomach, 'the old ones' was hardly a pin-point-accurate description of when I was best-off slipping these new ones (which he tells me are coloured bright red) down my gullet without running the danger of turning into a tube of bloody Smarties. He looked at me as if I were having a caesar, smiled politely, and hoped that I would manage as admirably as ever. Just like varnish, that one: once applied and dried , nothing sticks to him.

Now there you are, you see: I TOLD you not to let me get tangenital! Where was I? Oh yes: Christmas shopping. I've decided not to buy presents, this year, so don't go giving the postman earache because mine's not arrived. Now, if you're suffering from this annual migraine, yourselves, let me sooth your troubled brows. Just chat amongst yourselves and divi-out the following for me: a bottle's always welcome and a new pair of slippers (no bloody pom-poms, this time, mind you,) would save me from being crippled for the rest of my life – short though that may be. At this age, it's not worth asking for any more than's absolutely necessary.

I've no plans for New Year. I used to pop next-door but it's all-change, there, let me tell you. 52 years they'd been married to the best of my knowledge and to go off, just like that! It makes you think, doesn't it? I mean to say, women of her age should know better - and him but a slip of a lad. Of course, I could go around and sit with Mr. Slaughterthwaite but it's not easy to recruit a willing wallflower on festival occasions, and a solo visit would be unthinkable. Someone suggested I invite him round to mine. "Are you out of your mind?" I asked. "I'll have you know that since Mr. Arbuthnott's passing, the only single male anteloper to my house has been the man who reads the meter - and I'm not sitting with the front door open, all bloody night, in the middle of winter!" That told them.

Which brings me towards the end of my second side. I do believe in covering both, so to start a fresh sheet would be a waste as I've certainly not got enough to cover two more sides with. As you know, I've always preferred to keep my thoughts to myself, anyway.

As one more year smuggles towards the next,

Elsie Arbuthnott (Two ts, mind, not just the one.)

With the air of a Parliamentarian who has just resolved the Brexit *impasse*, single-handedly, Mrs. A. folded the letter neatly and placed it carefully into an envelope, which she sealed and addressed, ready to slip into the nearest post-box, next time she was out and about. That she placed no stamp upon the envelope may have been meanness, or forgetfulness, or simple practicality. After all, it was addressed to: *Santa & All His Elves, North Pole.*

Found Boy, Lost

{With acknowledgements to William Golding's *Lord Of The Flies.*}

His name was Percival Wemys Maddison. Not an easy name to forget. And yet, for a long time, it appeared that he had, himself, done precisely that. We have evidence that he had known it, at one time. Also, his address and telephone number. This was confirmed by one of the eldest within the group of boys which was rescued from an otherwise uninhabited island. Each of them needed some immediately physical and, subsequently, psychological care, but this strange little boy (probably four-rising-five) seemed to be the most emotionally damaged of all. He stared, dry-eyed, and silent. Silent, that is, apart from one, constantly repeated word: "I'm." He would move towards me, almost boldly, almost with a sense of determination. He would take me by the hand, and look directly at me, and then, with an assertiveness that belied his tiny physique, he would say ('announce' might be a better word) "I'm.......". The silence which followed was no termination of his sentence, but it was its finality. Sometimes, his lips would move, but they formed no coherent nor repeated shape. They released no sound; not even the merest suspiration of a whisper. They were as barren as his dry, staring, inexpressive eyes.

The Naval Officer who had rescued the boys, having spotted from afar the smoke rising from their once lush, now scorched, island, confirmed that, upon landing on its shore, he had been approached by the youngster. He, too, had been taken by the hand, engaged eye-to-eye, and assertively addressed. "I'm," the wee lad had boldly announced. Then no more had followed, other than mouth shapes, resembling those of a landed fish. Subsequently, a fair-haired youth, named Ralph, had confided that the small boy's name was "Percival Wemys Maddison; he told us on a number of occasions. He told us his address and telephone number, too. But I can't remember them. We didn't take that much notice of him, really."

They were all brought to my hospital. Their bodies were badly blistered from the sun; there were minor cuts and bruises that required attention; and they were of course, sufficiently exhausted to require much sleep. Slowly, their bodies healed, and their youthful energy was restored. It was evident, however, that there had been damage to much more than their soft tissue.

A red-headed boy, Jack, intrigued me. He, Ralph, and Roger were much the same age. As the Naval Officer had reported, Ralph appeared to have adopted the role of leader of the group. But Jack's reticence seemed to me to be unnatural. Just as Ralph appeared to be reasonably open, informative to a degree, half-willing to confide, Jack was as tight-shut as an oyster. Yet his manner was by no means meek. Were he to be powered by steam, I would have anticipated some form of burst, or explosion. That he volunteered as little as he could did not convince me that he was without either opinion or memory. Roger, also, troubled me. Troubled me more than Jack, in fact. If Jack were a pressure-cooker, Roger seemed to be something far more primitive. Knowing how normal teenaged boys are so keen to spar and to banter their way into superiority, Roger and

Jack's acceptance of Ralph's position within the group's pecking-order seemed to me to be suspiciously unnatural.

As soon as I had started to see each boy separately, I felt concerned. I asked each of them the same question: "Are you able to tell me the name of the small boy who says nothing but 'I'm'?" Ralph had immediately volunteered the information previously mentioned. Jack and Roger claimed no knowledge, at all. Nor did they volunteer any information about how the group had set about establishing themselves, following the air crash that The Ministry of Defence had been able to confirm, explaining the boys' presence, alone, on the island. Ralph had told me about their hut-building efforts, about how they had attempted to keep their camp-site clean, about the beacon they had lit to attract passing shipping or aircraft, about the way that Jack had organized hunting groups to secure meat, and about how they had done their best to cook it. Neither Jack nor Roger was prepared to comment. The one looked evasive; the other impassive. All three, it seemed to me, were withholding; internalising; increasing their trauma, rather than allowing it to be released.

There were, of course, other children in the group. Many were even younger than my monosyllabic patient and, it seemed to me, their best treatment, unless they exhibited more complex presentations, was fresh-air, and gently supervised freedom. But Ralph, Jack, Roger, and, most especially, the unwillingly silent Percival Wemys Maddison were cause for my considerable concern.

I saw each of the boys about whom I was especially troubled every day for an hour. Initially, that hour with Ralph passed quickly. During the first few days of this procedure, he seemed to be quite at ease. He had good recall of their initial days on the island; he presented a somewhat better-than-may-be-believed picture of their natural resilience and efficiency but, given that he was the accepted leader, this seemed quite natural. Then, suddenly, he had no more to add. He offered no further details; my attempts to solicit them failed. His hour started to become as elongated and unyielding as those given to Jack and to Roger.

The latter two had both started along the lines of, "Can't remember much, really. It's all a bit of a haze. Too much sun, I expect." It was almost as if they had devised a mutual strategy. This engendered two mutual concerns within me: how can I help them, if they will not open-up to me? What are they so ashamed of that forces them not to open-up? Ralph's own suddenly taciturn manner further fuelled these concerns. Might Percival Wemys Maddison be my more effective conduit? If so, how might I penetrate his mono-logism?

One day, he arrived to see me, exactly as had become his habit: on time, expressionless, silent, other than the occasional outburst of, "I'm ...." Eventually, I had to acknowledge that this approach had failed. He was the last to see me, on that particular day. I decided to foreshorten our hour's meeting in my clinic and to ask him if he would like to take a ride. Whilst exhibiting no great enthusiasm, he made no protest. And so we set-off.

I have often noted that children respond much more readily to animals than to adults. Close-by, there was one of those farms especially geared-up for visiting youngsters: small animals and lots of them recently-hatched, recently-born. It could be no less effective than my more normal approach had been. As we entered, collecting tasty nibbles to offer the young creatures, Percival retained his impassive gaze. I encouraged him to throw some chicken pellets to the tiny and fluffy bantams. With trained obedience, he obliged, but he exhibited no enthusiasm, nor excitement. Neither the lambs, nor the calves fared any better. The delightful Pygmy Goat kids that would have melted any youngster's heart lolloped by, as if they were invisible. The child never smiled, never sought to stroke, nor to cuddle any of these creatures. And he never looked at me. I had said that we should visit each pen; he obeyed. "So much for inventiveness," I thought, regretting my radical change of approach in the treatment of traumatised children.

We then passed through a Pets' Corner: rabbits and guinea-pigs, finches, canaries, and budgerigars; mice, hamsters, and gerbils. Not a flicker. As we moved out of the covered area and, I imagined, towards the exit, there was one further pen to see. Pigs are happier in the open air than indoors. I had felt that the experiment had failed when, suddenly, Percival's attention became arrested. So far, he had passed-by everything, impassively, distributing food without interest. Now, he stopped. Arrested. Galvanised, almost. He looked at the animals; he looked at me. He looked about and spotted some pig-nuts, at which he made an enthusiastic grasp. He leaned over the fence, distributing his handful of food with far greater diligence than he had chucked corn at the chickens, or dropped sunflower seeds into the finch cages. Until now, I had been more director than detector. But I noted the almost instant change of interest.

In the pen was a fat sow, which had recently farrowed. Battling for a teat apiece was a multitude of squealing, squirming piglets. The boy was entranced. "Do you like the piggies, then?" I enquired.

I have never been so shocked in my life.

The scream was more than piercing; it was primeval. It silenced the squeals of the piglets, and the contented grunts of their mother. It terrified me. I had heard no human being emit any such sound, before. I hope to, never again. It was, indeed, more porcine than human. It had about it something of the slaughter-house. I've never been to a slaughter-house. Nor, thank God, have I ever witnessed human slaughter - but, if I had, this is the disembodied eldritch I would expect to hear. It froze me.

And then I realised that the boy had jumped into the pen. Clumsy though this manoeuvre may have been, he intended no harm. He lay down in the slurry, cradling the sow's head and making no attempt to impede the piglets' feeding. He cradled the head and, strangely, the sow made no attempt to display that creature's inherent maternal aggression. Rather, it wallowed, granting access to the boy.

And then, he looked directly at me. "I'm ....I'm ....I'm........". Ten, maybe a dozen times, he uttered it. Each time, with increased urgency. Each time, struggling to add further words, but failing. It was a form of convulsion. And all the time, he cradled the sow's head. With a kind of manic devotion.

I attempted authority. "Percival, come out of the pen!" I ordered. "Percival: that's your name you know. You're Percival Wemys Maddison; that's who you are. Tell me! Tell me, yourself, who you are! Speak the words: 'I'm Percival Wemys Maddison.' Acknowledge your selfhood! Tell me; tell me NOW!"

He didn't respond. Or, rather, he did, but not in the way I had anticipated. He sedulously ignored me. He held the sow's head firmly in his hands, lifting it so as to address it, directly. And he began to speak. "Hallo, Piggy," he said. His articulation was as clear as any toddler-about-to-go-to-school's could be. "Hallo, Piggy. I'm so, so sorry."

The eyes that had remained stubbornly dry for months suddenly welled-up and overflowed. "You knew my name, Piggy. You knew all of us little'uns. You listened. You thought. You understood. You were braver than Simon. He knew. He tried to tell them but he was too shy. You knew, too. They wouldn't listen to you, but you kept trying to tell them. It made no difference. They did for you, just like they did for Simon." He paused. He stroked the sow's head, and she grunted, appreciatively. His focus and concentration both increased. "I know who you are - and you know who I am, don't you?" A pause. "That's right. I'm, I'm, I'm:" and then, spilling-out like projectile vomit, "I'm Percival Wemys Maddison. The Vicarage, Harcourt St Anthony, Hants." Another pause. Mournfully, "I used to know my telephone number, as well, but that was a long time ago. Before.

Before. …… ." But it was too soon for him to recall what had twisted his warped grasp of the world. In time, the details would be reclaimed; but it was a cicatrise which would never fade. It was an ugly welt upon his consciousness. And I had no salve to soothe it.

SUCH A SAD SIGHT

What was once Mothering Sunday has become Mothers' Weekend. Saturday found me amongst the first wave of celebrants. Two tables already occupied; one reserved. One of the established groups was plainly at ease; they were enjoying themselves in a perfectly natural manner. Evidently, they were in frequent social contact. The other group was making a good fist of it. "Conversation" tended to be a relay of extended monologues which had been carefully prepared in advance of the occasion but, quite clearly, 'communication' was their determined aim.

"Reserved" is an adjective suitable for the third table, A white- haired lady in a wheelchair but fit enough to step out of it, so that she may take her place at table. She arrived, beaming, and accompanied by two copper-haired attendants. Brother and sister? Husband and wife? Cousins? Who knows? Certainly, the old lady's hair did not have that tobacco-stained hint of a former red-head. Nor did their pug noses match the strong face of their guest, who was (without much ceremony) dumped on a bench seat. Any of the three chairs would have been more appropriate for her age and comfort!

She was then deserted, as the wheel chair was removed and orders at the bar were placed. This took almost ten minutes. Eventually, three sets of serviette-wrapped utensils were thrown onto the table by the man. The elderly lady carefully arranged them into place settings. A pint, a glass of wine, and half-a-pint of lemonade appeared. The pair disappeared to the carvery to secure food. Three plates of food having been delivered, eating commenced. It was all that commenced: no eye-contact; no verbal exchange; three folk eating alone at a table together.

Was the old lady deaf or, even daft? Ready communication with waiters and waitresses would say, “Absolutely not!” Was she curmudgeonly, ungrateful, a complainer? Not at all. Silently, she ate her meal with relish, clearing her plate. “You all right?” A question from the woman, but sounding more like an accusation than solicitousness. “Grand, thanks.”

The ‘couple’ began to converse. Almost in whispers, as if to isolate their guest even further. The old lady (more sharp-eared than may have been expected) grabbed a strand of the exchange and hauled herself into it. The woman looked at her and uttered the monosyllable, “No.” Her eyebrows were raised; a silent interlocution of expression with the man followed, and silence re-descended.

I didn’t wait to hear if a hypocritical enquiry of, “Have you had a nice Mothers’ Day lunch?” completed the occasion. It may just have choked me!

Let The Train Increase Your Pain

I had assumed that the booking frustration would be the end of it. Wrong! Just the beginning. Try booking a ticket, on-line, to Stratford-Upon-Avon. You will fail. Stratford (Int) & Stratford Parkway: no problem. U following P, your desired destination peaks out of the bottom of the drop-down menu, but it cannot be highlighted. Any attempt to reach it results in an automatic selection of Stratford (Int). Not only is it not where you wish to go; it costs a damn sight more! You can try re-booting, or re-locating, or re-trying. You are wasting your time. You cannot pre-book Stratford-Upon-Avon; a computer program (*sic*) will not let you.

But the queue to buy an in-station ticket is not *that* long and the loss of early-booking discount isn't *that* great and you're going to reach the platform *just* in time to board the train, so *who's* quibbling?

As it turns-out, the rush and the decision that there is insufficient time to buy a coffee is automatically neutralised by the announcement that the train you have strained every muscle to catch is delayed by 10 minutes, anyway. It's a kind of built-in safeguard. Of course, you now have time to buy that much-needed coffee. And you do. But there's nowhere to sit in the on-platform cafe, given the build-up (or should that be back-up?) of frustrated passengers already stranded on platform 6. But coffee has been yours for the purchasing. Which is good, given that you didn't have time at home, before you left to catch the bus that would ensure you reached the station in time to catch the train that is delayed.

Some of our journeys depend upon connections. Connections are pre-planned; they are not designed to accommodate delays. Thus, that ten minute late start, if you need to walk cross-city in order to link with your on-going transport, may be the preamble to further power-walking, scampering, even running (if you are fit enough to run cross-city without dropping.) A stimulation to the heart, (which we are told is good for us, just as long as it does not fell us) that we could forgive were it to result in our just leaping aboard the next stage of our journey, in order to keep to our schedule. Not so, if the breath-taking tilt results in a monitor informing us that the train we have bust a gut to catch is, itself, delayed by twenty minutes.

And, thus it is that we arrive at Stratford-Upon-Avon, which is where we wanted to arrive, and only twenty minutes later than intended, which is really neither here nor there. Is it?

Possibly not, until one begins to negotiate the return journey but a few hours later.

That's right: the 1503 is delayed until 1520. And then 1530. A little later, still, until 1540. And then it arrives, so all is well. Or is it? I wish to return to Birmingham and my wish is to be granted; not so those who had hoped to alight at one of ten stops designated on the schedule: this train has suddenly become "straight-through". Those who had contemplated Solihull, or Adcock's Green, for example, must get off this train, now, and await further information. But I'm on a roll: Moor St.

beckons. And then a moderately short walk to New St. Then home. Other than New St., upon arrival, has become a reception centre for ill-news from all cardinal points. The Virgin train to Euston has been cancelled, altogether; Cross-Country trains to Sheffield, Manchester, Edinburgh, Nottingham via Derby, ... ALL are subject to delayed departures. These announcements take-on an hallucinatory potency such that I become convinced that I have heard that my own train's delayed departure is in consequence of "... a late start from Aleppo." And a very reasonable explanation it seems to be, until the re-run clarifies that it is not Aleppo but 'the depot' from which one's looked-for engine has been slow to depart.

But, no matter. It's on its way and geared-up for collecting us from platform 7a, to which we migrate, *en masse*. Alas, it later becomes clear that, in fact, platform 11a is the place to be and an announcement makes clear, in schoolmasterly tones, that we are to make our way from one to t'other "as swiftly as possible, in order to prevent further delay" - as if *we* had been responsible for the twenty minute late departure, already, and we deserved reprimand should this become extended to twenty-one minutes!

"This train is comprised of 3 carriages." Three carriages; now nearing 5.00 p.m., and earlier delays to take into account. Cosy, certainly; too close for comfort? Decidedly. Contrary to Health and Safety Regulations? I would imagine it to be the case, without doubt.

"We apologise for an extended delay to the Cross-Country service to Nottingham via Derby; we are just awaiting the arrival of a group of passengers from

Cardiff." I cannot help myself from vocalising my immediate thought: "I hope to God they've left bloody Cardiff, by now!" Further attempts to turn human beings into tinned anchovies indicates that they are, now, amongst us.

But, hey, we're on our way! Slowly. There is a very long, heavily laden freight train immediately ahead of us. By now, anything approximating to "on time" is less past history and more pure fiction.

As I alight at my destination and head for the exit, I hear the following announcement: "We regret to announce that the new high-speed connection to Leeds is currently running eighteen minutes late." And, then, I espy a promotional poster: "Tell us what is wrong, and we'll put it right!"

A corporate pipe-dream. It's almost touching, in its naivete.

"I'M ALL BOXED-IN!"

The small congregation filed down the nave of the church, following and taking their time from the portly vicar, who led them. Though they were but few, it had been a full-blown service. The vicar's tradition was so high that it almost required oxygen for his flock to breath with ease. Quite possibly, his overly enthusiastic swinging of the censer and the resultant white-outs of incense added to this heady experience. Certainly, his yards of personal lace would have taken someone (and one doubts himself) hours of painstaking ironing. The late lamented Archbishop Laud, himself, would have been in a state either of admiration or of furious jealousy. Then there was the cope and the biretta, the crisply pressed cuffs, held in place by perfectly bowed and elaborately embroidered bands, and the shoes. Not, of course, Cardinal shoes. He was neither of that rank nor of that tradition. But shoes so supple, and shiny, and suitably metal-tipped to create a rhythm close to tap-dancing, as he sashayed from altar to great west door.

It had not been a Latin mass, but the register of language used required an arcane knowledge of Early Tudor English. And it had been a service of substance. The rite aside, there had been eulogies, a learned sermon, extensive (or do I mean extended?) prayers for "our late sister's soul", for the souls of those who had passed in recent months, for the souls of those of us left living and carrying the flame, for our Monarch and (individually nominated) her immediate family, for the Archbishops of Canterbury and of York, for the

Episcopate, for all clergy and lay-servants of The Church, for our Government, and Governments world-wide, for Captains of Industry and members of the Armed Services, for parents and teachers, and all others with responsibilities to the young, for the Police and those working within the Law to keep our society peaceful, regulated, and safe, for Doctors and Nurses, Surgeons, Anaesthetists, and Hospital Administrators, for Social Workers, for Local Government Councillors, for butchers, for bakers, and for candle-stick makers. Then had come memories of the deceased's parents, "devoted servants of this ancient church, who carried-on the traditions established by" an extraordinarily lengthy list of worthies, stretching-back many generations and well beyond the recollection or awareness of even the most enthusiastic genealogist within the assembled company.

And so (and at long last) the stout priest gathered into his hands a small but elegant wooden box. He stood before the altar, raising the box high above his head, genuflected in an exhibition of unexpected athleticism, turned (the box still aloft), and began his procession towards the grave-yard. Solemn step, by solemn step.

A grave, long grassed-over, had been re-opened. The sexton would be able to tell you that it contained two coffins, one some ten years older than the other. The lately deceased's parents'. Their child was to be returned to them. Slung in a form of bosun's chair constructed out of the vicar's stole, the wooden casket was lowered until it rested atop the uppermost coffin. Swiftly, rather like the table-cloth trick leaving the cutlery, crockery, and glassware perfectly positioned when the material has been whisked away, the casket rested, and the stole was replaced around the clergyman's shoulders. Now that he was fully attired, once more, he could commence his final prayers. And he did. Nor was he scant in prayerful regard.

Finally, boards and a cloth were laid over the open grave. It would be re-filled-in, later. The company moved away and towards the village inn, which had been expecting their arrival for some time. Happily, cold collation does not spoil.

And, there we shall leave them, these mourners and their memories. Let's return to the graveyard. A couple of brawny blokes are shovelling earth back into the chasm. We're on heavy clay and there has not been rain for several weeks. Even taking the top off this well-established grave was heavy work, earlier in the day. Replacing it is no lighter nor easier a task. But they fall to it with good will.

Passers-by can hear the crisp scrape of shovel upon dry and ston-hard earth. There is limited birdsong and the occasional lowing of a cow or whinnying of a horse. An occasional curse escapes the lips of our brawny pair. Otherwise, it is remarkably quiet.

Quiet enough for you and for me to hear a faint voice: *What the bloody hell have they put me in here for, the sanctimonious sods? They know damn well that I ran away from home, years ago, to escape these two narrow-minded, bigoted and tight-fisted buggers! WHY, after half-a-century's freedom, would anyone think that I wanted to spend eternity in a box, in a grave, and with these two? I'd rather have ended-up on a public refuse tip!*

The wake is in full-swing. The portly vicar is becoming portlier, still. An uplifting service has been conducted; spiritual reunion has been achieved; the traditions of a remote English village have been upheld.

Oy, is anyone listening? Oh, sod it! How am I going to sort this bloody mess out, then? Hallo: is there anybody there, damn it!? A ghostly voice, echoing through the void of an otherwise deserted graveyard.

A Fresh Recruit?

"So sorry, mate; I've really been talkin'; I *do* apologise."

"No sweat bruv! We sometimes 'ave to give it some, innit."

I was on my way from the train station to the bus stop I use, once my usual route home has closed-down, after 6.30 p.m. At this time of year, it has started to go dark by then, meaning that one, particular, shop entry (deeply-set-back-steps, good for both gathering-space and wind-sheltering convenience) will be populated. Only the early arrivals, at this time, of course. Closer-quarters are not kept until much later, much darker, much colder.

No, it was the phraseology that caught my ear, as I passed: "So sorry", "I *do* apologise". The "So" and the "*do*". Are you with me? Even the rhythmic structure. You don't need to *see* punctuation to know it's there. Or, indeed, not there. "Mate", of course, has become *lingua franca* amongst the young, but a well-tuned ear can tell whether or not it's common or coddled usage. Just the same with a present participle's dropped 'g'. Pains, like me: teachers; we can tell!

Then there was the timbre of the boy's voice. I say, 'boy'; it's a catch-all term. So, let's be more specific: this 'young man', if you prefer, would be late-teens. Ex-Sixth Form (just), I'd say. Remember: we're focussing on tone, not accent, here. It had clarity. His delivery was not, yet, shredded by cheap booze and roll-ups. The same could not be said of his responder. Hardly any older (possibly, even, not as old) but with a voice-box already peeling. As if a rasp had been forced down his gullet, the soft sides of which had been pierced and pulled by that rasp's withdrawal.

Don't get me wrong. I'm not being judgemental, here. Observational. Enquiring. That's what I'm trying to be. There can be no doubting the sympathy and support offered by the husky-voiced, less schooled bloke. The one with the still-choir-boy-clarity admits that he's been banging-on a bit and, obviously, the Artful Dodger to Oliver has patiently listened. Having listened, he could have said something along the lines of, "Hey, kid, get real. You has choices; some of us ain't. Take you pick and stick, man, but quit whingeing." No such objection was made. "I know where you at" was the essential response. And I'll tell you what: that Artful Dodger/Oliver bit may have been unfair. Dickens's Dodger is out to catch innocents; to peddle them to Fagin. To pimp them. The Artful becomes cheeky-chappie-charming, as Jack Wilde falsely presents him to be in "that" film! Dickens knew the back streets of London, alright. There again, the comparison may be spot-on. All armies, no matter what their cause, need recruits. Sensible Generals don't ask questions.

As well as hearing this brief exchange, as I passed, I also noticed the spliff, nursed in the (mostly) innocent's right-hand. Was he naturally loquacious, or had chemistry played a part in his having "... really been talkin'..."? I've no idea. And, anyway, who am I to say? Indeed, what's it to me?

Undoubtedly, during the early-darkening hours of this winter, I shall pass that shop entrance, frequently.

Certainly, there will be gatherings within it that grow, as late afternoon becomes early evening, passing on to night-time. And then there will be dawn. I will never be sure if that clarion-voiced, grammatically accurate, distinctively phrased speaker is amongst the groups that shelter there. Almost certainly, if he is, it will become increasingly difficult to distinguish him. His natural voice. But it won't stop me from wondering.

"Is It Worth It?"

His arrival in my carriage was announced by a grunt, bordering on a groan, as he removed the tight gloves and plastic helmet which identified him as a cyclist. An identification increased by his shorts, with a protruding inch of lycra under-support. A big man, both tall and bulky, he dropped into his seat, releasing an expressive sigh, followed by a pained moan. With his hands he then dry-washed his face in that way we all do, when utterly exhausted. It was close on midnight, after all.

"That good a day, then?" I felt forced to respond. He just shook his head, which he allowed to hit the back cushioning of his seat, closed his eyes, and sighed once more.

"Is it worth it, I wonder?" This partly to himself and partly in reply. Heavily accented: Eastern European, probably, but bleared by a mixture of extreme weariness and genuine self-doubt.

He had been on his bike for nine hours. Not a challenge, nor a charity marathon, but a cost-reducing attempt to earn some money. Hired, no doubt, by some organization or another expecting too much and paying as little as the law will permit. I didn't ask for details, recognising that an animated exchange was beyond him, altogether. He did, however, volunteer that he had earned £75. £13 of that had now disappeared on his train fare home, for he could pedal no further. Inevitably, he then dozed-off.

It was a stopping train. One station was succeeded by another, at regular ten minute or so intervals. Ought I to have enquired where he was heading before he had fallen asleep? Should I nudge him before the next stop, just in case? But he opened his eyes, and noted that his stop was the next along the line. Its approach was announced. He replaced his cycling gloves and safety-helmet, eased his aching body from his seat, and walked to collect his bike, bidding me a good night. "Hope you're home and in bed, very soon," I responded.

The train stopped. I took no notice of sounds nor activities. I was growing weary, myself. The twenty minutes of largely unexplained stasis, just shy of Leicester, had added unwelcome length to a round trip that had started over twelve hours earlier. After a couple of minutes, we were back in motion.

Then, a recently familiar sigh. "My" cyclist slumped into the seat he had only just vacated. Arms were crossed on the table; his head was placed upon their cushion; a combination of frustration and despair was expelled. He looked across the aisle, raised his hands into the air, and said, simply, "Doors no open."

A sudden shock of guilt re-invigorated me. "Damn!" This route was familiar to me; I should have warned him; it just had not occurred to me, in my own bleariness. His station has a short platform; we were in the rear carriage; its doors would have remained secure. I *knew* this! *What* an imbecile I was not to have warned the poor man! But, hold on. There had been no regular warning. "The next station has a short platform; those in carriage A who wish to alight at this station should move forwards to carriage B." I had heard it so often, before. But, tonight, I had absolutely no recollection of that essential announcement. Apologetically, I explained what must have happened. He was adamant in his agreement that there had been no announcement.

He then applied himself to his mobile phone. Another anguished sound was emitted. At the next station, our terminal destination, ours was to be the last train in or out until the following morning.

My sense of injustice was activated. This was wrong. It was not his own fault that he was about to be faced with yet another hour or so on his bike, or a ruinously expensive taxi fare home. I urged him to seek-out the guard and to protest. A combination of his physical exhaustion, his limited English, and an inertia brought on by unequal odds left him sitting in his seat and staring into space. He'd had enough for one day.

"We are now approaching our final destination. I repeat: this is our last stop. All change, please; all change!" And the doors of our carriage slid open.

"Hold on," I said. Let's go and explain to that bloke, over there." And I gently propelled the man and his bike towards a uniformed official. I explained that the announcement, instructing him to move forwards in the train, had not been made. Implacably, he responded with that bureaucratic intonation that can be *so* irritating, "Your train was composed of four carriages." Nothing further; just this fact. Even when I repeated the complaint, he merely parried by repeating his explanation. I pushed for further clarification. As if addressing a moron, he noted that four carriages would have fitted the short platform, so the announcement was not needed, and all doors would have been released.

"But *that's* precisely my point: they *weren't* !"

With a fluency that implied this was not the first time he had encountered such a contradiction, his automaton voice instructed us to find the Station Supervisor, who was located on another platform, and to report our complaint to him. And he walked, unperturbed, away from us to close the carriage doors of the now-empty train.

Up a flight of stairs. A few yards along the flat. Down a flight of stairs. Where, on this seemingly deserted platform, might we find the Station Supervisor? It was now 0035; I had initially caught the 1137, as I had set-out for my busy day. Even by that time, the man had been on his bike for hours, already. He must, by now, be totally exhausted.

"And what might I do to help you two gentlemen?" A booming voice. Eccentric in timbre, to the point of seeming to belong either to a Music Hall artiste or to the ghost of a long-dead Station Master of old. From the shaded far end of the platform emerged a figure of considerable bulk. He did not loom, for there was something more comforting about his presence than that. Nor did he lumber, for he carried his corpulence with neat precision; with, one might be tempted to suggest, balletic poise. As the voice and the vague outline materialised into sharper definition, we recognised an authoritative personality, costumed theatrically. He was in uniform, but either he had been granted special dispensation to retain one from an earlier era or his personality somehow informed his dress. It was redolent of the steam era. A face, rubicund even in the acid light cast onto the platform, was framed by carefully-tended mutton-chops, themselves united by an undulating moustache. It was a contrivance that could only be described as being 'braggadocio'.

Once again, I rehearsed my vicarious tale of woe. He listened. He neither interrupted, nor did he advance a contrary version of the events he had not witnessed. "Foreign gentleman, far from home?" he enquired of me, inclining his head towards the man with the bike. I explained that he was; that he had basic English but that he was exhausted, and I had, thus, volunteered myself as spokesman. "And most generous of you, too, sir; if I may say so. I suggest that we repair to my office, where we shall find a modicum of comfort, warmth, and hot coffee. Kindly follow me." So, we did.

His office mirrored the man's dress and manner. 'Anachronistic'; that's probably the best word. Within and in addition to the utilitarian work space, there was as much junk-shop-rescue-soft-furnishing as would fit. Certainly, sufficient to seat three. Its walls were covered by a curiously controlled riot of artefacts. All of them tat but, within this context, homely; comforting. On a hotplate, and as promised, rested a large, gently steaming, dull-metalled coffee-pot. From its spout arose not merely steam but scent. The scent of a rich, reviving brew. Its taste was true to its fragrance.

"Now, gentlemen: here, we are presented with a conundrum. And, as is the case with all conundra (which I believe to be the classically correct pluralisation), a resolution is required. Alas, I can proffer you nothing either immediate or adequate, for I am not authorised to decide upon cases of compensation – and, indeed, even if I were, all such cases adjudicated in favour of the appellant are reimbursed, retrospectively."

Whilst the coffee was both comforting and reviving, the Supervisor's nineteenth century novel-like oratory, vaguely amusing though it might be, was extremely frustrating.

"Couldn't he just kip down here overnight and catch the first train, tomorrow?" I interjected, reining-in his wordy, if impressively fluent, overview of the situation.

"That, Sir, is a proposal seemingly logical in its approach but wholly at odds with regulations. When I depart, the station will be in lock-down until my worthy assistant arrives in several hours' time and in order to restore its operative mode. His discovering an intruder would necessitate summoning the Railway Constabulary. A course of action I could not possibly allow myself to be party to, alas. And now, Sir," turning his attention to the cyclist, "if I could furnish you with this documentation via which your claim may be submitted, in accordance with the instructions provided, I fear I must be on my way. As, indeed, must you be, too." A folded A4 sheet and self-addressed envelope were passed over, and the Supervisor opened the door of his office, bidding us both farewell and fair fortune. His olde-worlde charm had run its course.

Outside the station lurked two taxis. Light drizzle was giving way to more persistent rain. "Thank you for your efforts," the man said, presenting a hand to be shaken. He placed his folded bike inside the more capacious taxi of the two, closed the door behind him, and set-off on his journey home. Evidently, the prospect of yet another hour or so, cycling in increasingly bad weather, was beyond his remaining resources. I boarded the other taxi, which would take me in the opposite direction. How much of his now £62 earnings for that long day's work would remain, after he had paid his fare, I wondered. It was an extremely depressing thought. Certainly, it set his own earlier question echoing in my mind: "Is it worth it, I wonder?"

"Let's Not Tell Mummy"

Saturday lunch-time: it's when estranged parents meet their offspring. This set-up's pretty typical: 4ish year old daughter; early 30s dad. She is playing hard to get; he is trying far too hard, altogether.

"What would you like to eat?" he asks.

"I don't know."

"Well, shall I read-out what there is?"

"Yes please." So sweet; so insincere!

He's using that "special" voice. Not the one we hear, as he responds to his many phone calls; this one's "the daddy voice": light, soft, faux-patient; his aim is that it will last for the rest of the afternoon. Then, it'll be another fortnight before he needs to make the effort, again.

"Well now, let's see. Would you like a toasted-sandwich, or a baked potato, or WHAT ABOUT A PIZZA!?" Each is made to sound irresistibly flavoursome. Each is declined, with a carefully rehearsed pout and a wrinkled nose. "Perhaps you'd like a burger. Mummy doesn't do burgers, does she? That'd be a nice change for you. A TREAT!" Silence. Extended silence. "So, you don't fancy a burger, then? Never mind. Let's see what else there is to choose from, shall we? Ooh, I know: why don't we share? We could order a Daddy-sized dish and you could help Daddy to eat it. Does that sound nice?"

She is preoccupied with her new My Little Pony toy. The latest in a Yard-full of other soft, fluffy equines. Each adored for a day and then each put out to grass. Yet more clutter for Mummy to attempt to keep tidy. Such devotion obviates the need to pay attention to Daddy, who's becoming obsessed with ordering lunch.

"Now, Daddy could fancy any number of these lovely choices. Isn't it a great place to meet?" No response. "Don't you think?" Still no response. "When we've had our scrummy lunch, there's a soft-play area for you. That'll be fun, won't it?" Maybe it will; maybe it won't; the jury's out on this one.

"Anyway, back to choosing lunch. Perhaps you'd like to share a big All-Day- Breakfast. I know Mummy doesn't think that fried food is good, so you probably don't often get any lovely bacon, or scrummy sausages. And you could dip your hash-brown in the runny egg-yolk. That's what Daddy loved to do, when he was little, like you, and living with Granny and Grandad." Any possibility of a slightly delayed response is curtailed by a ring-tone. He checks his screen and then answers. "Hi, how're you doing? Us? Oh, we're just drooling over the lunch menu and trying to figure-out what we fancy most. No, not yet. She can't quite make her mind up. Well, there seems to be no great rush. Why not? That would be great. There's a soft-play area, which'll keep her occupied, once we've eaten. There's loads to choose from, so you're bound to fancy something. Now, now: none of that! Not yet, anyway. Ha! Great, see you in about ten or so. Byeee!"

Preoccupied with her toy though she has seemed to be, the little girl has also been attentive to the phone call. Much more attentive than she has been, thus far, to the menu options. "Is *she* coming, too, then?" Her tone is disturbingly grown-up; a pre-echo of the fourteen-year-old she will, one day, become. It quite wrong-foots him. An admonishment would not be inappropriate. But it's difficult both to admonish and to retain that special Daddy-voice he has promised himself to use, throughout. Mummy admonishes; she can be quite sharp, sometimes. Daddy's *much* gentler, much kinder, (much luckier to be a seven-hour-a-fortnight) disciplinarian.

"Auntie Sue? Yes, she'll be here in a few minutes. *Then* we'll choose what to eat and have a lovely lunch, together, before you have fun in the soft-play area."

It is not going well. Nor had it gone well the previous fortnight. To be frank, it's bloody hard work!

She continues to torture her new toy. He checks-out Facebook on his mobile.

And then 'Auntie Sue' arrives. As you will already have realised, she's no auntie at all; she's his latest squeeze. I say "latest" because he has the look of a serial operator about him. Of course, I have no proof. I don't even know him; never clapped eyes on him until he and his little princess occupied the adjacent table. I'm an observer, not a creator. But, more often than not, it's difficult to compartmentalise the two. Almost always, we observe creatively.

"Hi, you!" He adopts a casual, everything's-perfectly-normal stance. No hugs-and-kisses. No leaping-to-his-feet. Just an eyes-raised, "Hi, you!" She echoes his greeting, slips-off her coat, and occupies an empty chair. She's wearing a tastefully understated Jersey Wool dress: delicate dove-grey and decorated with a dusky-pink motif. Very chic; very expensive. "Look who's here!" he exclaims, with that Children's TV faux-enthusiasm that's moving from *interesting* to *irritating* on my own 'emotograph'. Quite deliberately, the little girl upgrades her casual disinterest to a patently deliberate ignoring. Her body swivels within the confines of her chair so that her back, not her face, is presented to Auntie Sue. And she opens-up an animated conversation with her toy. It's amazing quite how much a pink My Pony filly has to say for itself, once it gets started!

The adults exchange looks. His indicates annoyance; hers, acceptance. "Leave this to me!" he seems to be wanting to say; "Give it time", her eyes reply. She then begins to chat to him: which shops she's visited, that morning; what's taken her fancy, and what's so ridiculously expensive, these days. The lovely man in the jeweller's who was so helpful over her watch-strap, "and, hey-presto, here it is: good as new!" This relaxes him. His inclination to 'sort this out' segues into, 'she's only a kid'. He even manages to accept the conversational baton and to tell her about a chance call from an old associate who may well be able to put something his way. No promises, of course, but a good 70/30 possibility. Great stuff, if it were to come-off.

Time is passing. More and more tables are becoming occupied. There's even a short queue starting to form. Thus far, he's purchased one espresso and a high-in-e-numbers bottle of fizz (still half-full.) Thick-skinned he may be, but even he recognises that he cannot continue to use this facility as a form of creche for much longer. At least he can buy a bit more time via another coffee for himself and one for Sue. Or, damn it, *why not*? "Two large Pinot Grigios, please," he asks, once the waiter has been alerted.

The wine arrives. The two glasses are raised and chinked. "Cheers," they duet.

Suddenly, the little girl realises that no one has asked her if she wants anything. "I'm hungry," she whines. Inwardly relieved, he recites his earlier litany of dishes available.

"You two choose first," she says. All sweetness and light. As if butter wouldn't melt .... . The full charm offensive. He sticks with the All-Day-Breakfast; the lady-friend selects Fettuccini, in a creamy tuna and mushroom sauce. "I'd like to share with Auntie Sue," the child lisps. A quick exchange of adult eyes establishes that this is an acceptable arrangement. The order is given. The establishment's name is lived up to and their food arrives "B4 U Can Say Jack Robinson". Auntie Sue ladles about a third of her meal onto the little girl's empty plate, helpfully cutting the pasta ribbons into manageable lengths. It disappears almost as swiftly as it was delivered. "May I have some more, please, Auntie Sue?" An irresistibly cute request. As is its repetition, shortly afterwards. The intended two-thirds:one-third apportionment has been inverted.

Then, inevitably, "I feel sick!"

Sue whisks the child to The Ladies. It is some time before they re-emerge. Expansive wet patches on both their outfits indicate that it has not been an entirely neatly executed operation.

But she's a brave girl. She manages a sheepish smile. There are no tears.

Not, that is, until Daddy says, "Let's not tell Mummy about this."

Round Robin

(A festive folly.)

One frosty, late-November morning brought a shaft of piercingly strong sunlight into Robin's bedroom. Someone had drawn his curtains; curtains that had been closed for the past twelve months. So bright was the light that, reluctant though he was, Robin had to pay heed. With his eyes still tightly closed, he sighed deeply. This was no expression of contentment, nor of satisfaction with his uninterrupted (until now) year-long slumber. It was a sigh that betokened unwilling recognition. A sigh that almost spoke. Indeed, within Robin's head, it did speak. "It's *that* time of year again, your Rotundness," it whispered - and not without a hint of malice; a suggestion of ironic delight. "Time for you to be up-and-dressed; to be armed with inconsequentialities; to be sent around, once again"

"Oh no," thought a disconsolate Robin, "surely it's too soon." As if his words had been spoken aloud, they received a response. "*Never* too soon, your Tubbitude. Early arrivals expected Nov.29th and onwards."

Robin, who had indeed gained weight during his lengthy withdrawal from the world and its goings-on, reluctantly dragged himself off to the bathroom, where he conducted his annual ablution. Time, then, to be dressed. Round Robin's attire was not like yours and mine. Oh no! No cotton, cord, nor cardigan; no silk, no satin, no suede; nothing loosely thrown around his shoulders nor draped around his neck. Robin was swathed in paper. Sheet after sheet of paper. And all of it written upon. Some sheets were typed, some were handwritten; there was biro, cheap and nasty, blurred by blotches, and there was fountain-pen script (so much more elegant though not necessarily more legible), and, sometimes, there were photographic illustrations, too, - oh, and links. Links were the preserve of the word-processed pages. They were a way of making a short letter longer. Much longer!

Once he was fully dressed, Robin was not just round; he was globular! His stubby legs and his splayed, Mister-Men-styled feet, tottered beneath the weight of his epistolary excess and his foreshortened arms would certainly struggle to reach the earliest sheets of his delivery round. But he would not fail. Robin may have been built more for comfort than for speed, but he could be relied upon to fulfil his duty.

So off he set. He had news to spread. Auntie Florrie's bunions had given her a deal of trouble over the past 12 months and, to be honest, that walk to the polling station in June had set her back at least two months or so. I mean, had it been worth it, considering the outcome? She may just as well have stayed at home in her comfy slippers for what difference it had made. Had the grape vine caught-up, concerning a sudden outbreak of Japanese Knotweed in Uncle Archie's allotment? (Was "grape vine" acceptable, in the circs.? Or did it trivialise this really quite serious issue? Do let me know; I'd have re-written it, other than it may be considered quite witty by some. You just don't know, do you?) We're likely to hear a lot more about this, on account of 'the complications'. You see, whilst the leaves and stalks are incontrovertibly within the bounds of Archie's plot, the point of the plant's origin, given the straggly nature of roots, is subject to further enquiry. Indeed, as I write, an EGM of the allotment executive committee has been planned for next-Thursday-fortnight and the outcome may well go viral. Of course, we're not as many as we were. I'm reliably informed that 2nd -cousin-twice-removed Ethel's live-in-companion (male) has allowed his wheezy chest to get the better of him - *not*, of course, that Ethel, herself, has seen fit to let me know. But that side were always, how should I put it? Does 'not like our side' convey my meaning clearly enough? Anyway, be that as it may, you'll be interested to discover that our Barry's been promoted. Yes, that's right: *Barry/promoted*! After a decade as Assistant Salesperson (they're very politically correct, where he's at,) he's now been catapulted to the rank of *Senior* Assistant Salesperson. *That'll* give some detractors (I looked that one up and it fits, just grandly,) something to think about. Of course, the grand-children are a constant delight (in their way.) I had to laugh, the other day, when our Cedar (I mean, what kind of a name is that, I ask you?) was showing me his Tablet (oh, yes, I'm up with all the terminology) and he said to me, "Gran. what did you do when you were my age and the sun was shining really brightly?" Well, I started to tell him and then he interrupted me (not rudely but firmly) and said, "man that sounds so much hassle - especially when, nowadays, it's just a matter of drawing the curtain so you can still see the screen. Would you mind doing that for me, Gran.?" What really made me laugh was his calling me "man"; I think he gets so involved, sometimes, he doesn't remember who he's talking to - and, of course, his Grandad's not been with us these past 4 years. Anyway or not, we've all marvelled at young Indigo (another name I struggle with; I mean, if it's *that* end of the spectrum you're after, what's wrong with Violet? If it was good enough for Lady Grantham it's good enough for anyone. Unless, of course, you're a boy. But we might need to get onto that, later. So where was I? Oh yes, Indigo: she seems to be diversifying from her - did she call it a double-third? - anyway, she did very well in her degree about 'climaxology' I think it was; something to do with constant high-pressure and anti-cyclones, I remember her telling me. But I'm going off my tale. Mixed rugby; that's what she's going in for. Her mother says she's starting as a three-quarter but I'm sure, knowing that young lady's ambition, she'll be a four-fifths before we know it. I do have my worries about Cherokee, though. I told his mother, at the time, that no good would come of a silly name like that. "Tell that to an entire nation," was her sole response and what, I ask you,, was I supposed to make of that? Well, as you know, it resulted in me not going to Sunday tea for a good two months or so, until we buried the hatchet (oops - is that what they call a pun of sorts?) It was all well and good whilst he was little and I suppose "Chezza", which the others now call him, isn't as bad as his real name but I'll tell you truly: it's scarred him for life and no mistake. I was alerted to trouble a while back when he asked me something I didn't really take any notice of at the time. "Gran.," he said, in a strange kind of tone, "if you'd had the choice, would you have preferred to be a man?" Well, I told him straight, "I've always been happy in a nice floral print; you wouldn't see me dead in a donkey jacket!" And nothing more was said. But I can't help thinking that, maybe, he wasn't really asking about me. Oh, I know he's 14 and how 'alternative' teenagers are, these days, though I can't help but wonder if they're *all* quite as interested in make-up as he is. Anyway, I mustn't overstay my welcome and, as you can see, mine's an uneventful enough life, with little or nothing to report. So looking forward to news of you and yours and ever hopeful that the arthritis holds fire sufficiently for me to write again, next year.

Robin's round had been a long and tiring one but he had finally come to his last delivery. His girth had reduced considerably and he was moving with much greater ease. He popped his last sheet of paper through a letter box and began to walk home. He was in a quite reflective mood. "I wonder," he pondered, "how folk used to keep in touch in the PRR years? Or, maybe, they didn't. Maybe I'm not such a dollop as some folk make-out, after all." And, with that, he let himself back into his house, ate a satisfying supper, and prepared himself for a well-earned sleep.

“Not For Me, Thanks!”

We enter a sea-front restaurant in a popular English resort and at about one-fifteen. To my mind, it’s a decision of questionable good sense. Over-crowded, under-spaced, no draught beer! But I find myself to be in the minority. “How charming!” proclaims one companion; “Just perfect!” proclaims the other. “It’s not a pub,” I mumble, sulkily, and to no effect whatsoever.

We are approached by a waiter. “Table for three, lads?” Lads! I’m the youngest by nearly a decade and *I’m* sixty-four! Nonetheless, I find myself gathered, much in the way that a sheep-dog gathers a flock together, propelling it towards and then into the confined space of a holding-pen. “Not sure I can make it through that narrow gap; you can do it, though,” I am assured by one of my companions. The narrow gap refers to the space (if ‘space’ is quite the most apposite word) to describe the narrow channel between our designated table and that to which we are about to become juxtaposed. Heroically, I shimmy through. And, thus, I find myself facing into the rapidly filling restaurant, as the other two, seated rather more expansively, verbally applaud the seaward vista they are able to enjoy, rather than my prospect of heaving human flesh.

Breakfast at the hotel had been no menial affair. Although I had opted for kippers, rather than ‘Full English’, my plate had been loaded with four fillets of them. And, indeed, they had been delicious, as had been the wholemeal toast and marmalade; delicious, but extremely substantial. I am not hungry to *any* degree of the word. My ideal lunch would have comprised a pint a good beer and a small sandwich – no chips, no salad. Now I find myself looking at a menu advertising items that no doubt would be delicious but only to those needing a good, square meal. I am not up for even a paltry oblong one!

"What would you like to drink?" one of my companions asks.

"I would *like* to drink a pint of beer," I whine, "but it's either lager-on-tap or bottled, here. I don't like either, so I'll join you in whatever wine you've already decided on."

The wine arrives. Our food order is requested. I have noted that '*sandwiches, various*' are on offer; I have also spotted '*crab salad*'. "May I combine the bread of *sandwiches various* with the crab of *crab salad* in order to enjoy a crab sandwich?" I ask, believing that I am asking for nothing especially complicated (and, indeed, that "various" may include crab, anyway.)

"I'm afraid we do not offer crab sandwiches, sir. But I can recommend the crab salad."

"At £12.50 and presenting me with three times more than I will be able to eat, I've no doubt you can!" is my riposte. Voice light and humorous, rather than sharp and curt. "All I want is a simple sandwich and crab is the particular filling I fancy," I offer with the appealing look of a puppy mascot, encouraging folk to give generously.

But this waiter knows his lines. "I'm afraid we do not offer crab sandwiches, sir." Indeed, it is in danger of becoming his mantra!

"OK," I venture, still both patient and hopeful. "Do you serve bread and butter?"

"Yes, sir."

"So how would it be if I ordered bread and butter, requesting, as an indulgence, a dollop of crab meat, for which I am perfectly prepared to pay a reasonable sum? I make the sandwich and eat it; you tell me how much I owe."

"I'm afraid that wouldn't be possible, sir."

"No," think I, "that was always on the cards."

"Fine," I say but still with good cheer and explaining to my companions that I'm really not hungry at all. "No food for me, thanks." Thus, he retreats to the kitchen to place an order for two at the table for three.

There is something about this establishment that suggests that it is by no means a recent addition to the resort's facilities. Not that it is seedy in any way, nor that it fails to measure-up to current expectations of public hygiene. The décor is not faded, nor is there a general sense of torpor about the place: young waiters and waitresses, an utterly contemporary menu, clientele embracing the full age-range. No, what gives it that well-established air is the way in which it utilises space. Behind the crisp new paintwork and the faux-marble table-tops there lurks the previous Age of Austerity. Tables have occupied their current space since the Fifties. Different tables but the same space. The arrangement is based upon what would be considered comfortable by slender men in high-waisted trousers and hand-knitted, Argyll-patterned, tank-tops. Equally narrow-waisted women in pleated skirts, and disciplined children are the models for the ergo-dynamics of this establishment. Over half-a-century has passed. Austerity rules, once again, it is true, but it has gained a greater girth. As their meals arrive, my two companions become increasingly aware of this incontestable fact (no matter how big a spin on their choice of lunch venue they are attempting.)

One of them is buttressed against a wall, thus it is incumbent upon the other (who is, it should be noted, inclining towards the upper end of 'corpulent') to shuffle. And shuffle he does - way beyond the margin of our allotted table. Somewhat relieved, they settle into their chosen dishes. The table (for two) adjacent has remained unoccupied since our arrival. This status is not destined to last for much longer. Two ladies, one stout and the other stouter still, enter the restaurant. With pleasure, they spot the vacant table for two and make immediate headway towards it. As with our own arrival, the less substantial, more agile of the pair is elected to squeeze-by. Her display of calisthenics is accompanied by a chorus of, "It's a bit tight, but we're rate." Of course, you now know that we are on the East Coast of Yorkshire. Yorkshire folk, and Yorkshire women especially, do not suffer in silence. Thus, as the more matronly of the couple settles into her chair, she becomes aware that there is little less than a cigarette card's worth of unoccupied space between her and one of my companions. He, on the other hand, and perhaps distracted by the pleasure he is gaining from what he considers to be "a wisely selected dish, indeed", registers nothing of this.

"Ey up,": the unmistakable sound of Northern Woman roused; "I said, 'ey up'!" And she looks at him. "This is a bit close-up and comfortable, I'n't it?" At first, he is blissfully unaware that he is the person addressed; when he does realise, he totally misunderstands. He can read Old and Middle English and won a scholarship to Oxford, but Northern Woman has never been his area of interest nor expertise. He thinks that she is passing the time of day; that she is exhibiting that famous Northern Friendliness that he has read about in books.

"Oh, yes, indeed!" he eventually responds with a full (now extremely full) bellied chortle, and he re-directs his attention to his diminishing plate-full of food. He does not see fit to move his chair one centimetre away from her.

She looks at her friend and then pitches her voice a note higher, increasing her volume accordingly. "I was just saying, 'this is a bit close-up and comfortable', don't you think?"

"Well," replies her dining companion, indicating that a form of code has clearly been cracked, "As you say, *very* close-up and, erm, comfortable." Ostensibly, her remark is addressed across their table, but it is clear to me that its intended direction is inter-table.

I feel obliged to attract the attention of my companion. A gentle heel-hack, followed by a complex sequence of ocular Morse code follows. All this elicits is a smug, "You know, you *are* a silly sausage. This is a truly excellent dish!" Assuming that I'm in no mood to riposte, he re-directs his attention to his plate. Meanwhile, the lady who feels (not unreasonably) that her personal space has been invaded, begins to transmit her agitation via a series of physical demonstrations. They prove that Les Dawson was an observational genius for they precisely imitate his gyrations when in character as Northern Woman. Her dewlaps begin to wobble, her shoulders and what are called 'bingo wings', these days, shake involuntarily, hip-gyration causes her bottom to be in a state of agitation. I think I have suddenly become lucid in this particular dialect of body language. It is stating, and in no uncertain terms, "I don't want to have to say anything rude but, if needs must, *I bloody well will*!"

"I'm just popping upstairs," she says to her friend at a level of volume far in excess of necessity and with etched articulation.

"Right you are," her friend replies and, again, the unnatural emphases indicate that an attempt to alert my companion to his solecism is being made. No one wants a scene, but one is developing into an encounter as explosive as any freak summer thunderstorm.

Again, I do my best to help resolve the situation. "All the tables seem to be very tightly packed together," I venture. "It's very much a case of elbows in and don't spread, here, isn't it?"

"Oh, you're just sulking over the lack of beer. It's a perfectly comfortable and really rather sweet establishment. Do you think we should have some more *Pinot*?"

Upon her return, she exaggerates the process of lowering herself into her seat and then pronounces, emphatically, "Well, there's one thing to be said about this place: there's a bloody site more space in the lavvy than there is down 'ere!" There is a short pause. Nothing happens. My companions continue to sip their wine, oblivious to the mounting tension. I consider intervention. But I am too late. The woman's capacity for subtlety has reached its elastic limit. She half-turns in her seat, looks directly at him, extends her podgy hand towards his equally podgy shoulder, gives him a firm but unaggressive prod and states clearly, "Budge-up, duck; thee and me's faitin', ovver space, 'ere!"

At first, he can't quite believe this to have happened! His entire bulk freezes, the wine glass still half-way to his lips. My other companion, sitting to his right, looks at him anxiously, as if he fears the sudden on-set of Stroke. I cannot quite decide whether to laugh-out-loud, to attempt a UN-style intervention, hoping to create an atmosphere suitable to negotiations, or to make a bid for freedom by squeezing through the narrow space and heading for The Gents. "I beg your pardon, Madam?" I hear the words come spluttering from the lips that the wine glass has still failed to reach. Either she doesn't or chooses not to notice the rising inflexion and she takes the words to be a statement, rather than a question; an apology, not an expostulation.

"Granted, I'm sure!" she says, triumphantly. "Now let's both on us get us dinner ate, afore it gus cowd." And she proceeds to address her cod and chips. At our table, silence obtains. The wine glass's journey to his mouth remains in a state of arrest; the hue of his face moves through all the shades of darkening until, finally, reaching that of purple-close-to-black.

"Well, *really*!" he finally explodes. She chomps away blithely, as unaware of the incursion she has made into the territory of his dignity as had been he, concerning his invasion of her personal space.

"No grub ordered, lad?" she asks me, just before a slurp of tea, followed by a discreet burp.

"Not for me, thanks. I'm quite full, already!" I reply, thinking, contentedly, to myself, "I suspect that pint of beer's not that far-off, now."

Still Hard Times

"Oy, You, Sort That Mess Out For Me!"

BANG!

"Fuck me! I'm on fire!"

It had never been much of a garden. Several years of neglect and abuse had turned it into a near-midden. It was where the dogs crapped; where abandoned boxes were dumped; a parking lot for outdated toys. Unpruned shrubs marked its perimeter; unattended grass suggested a former lawn. She recognised that it was a mess. It needed sorting.

An old-fashioned bonfire offered the obvious start. But bonfires can be slow to burn - especially when not carefully constructed. A bonfire is more than a pile of kicked-together rubbish. It's a structure. It has design. The teenager instructed to sort-out the mess knew nothing about building bonfires. But he did like blazes. A haphazard pile of trash and a few screwed-up sheets of newspaper will burn. But slowly. And he's impatient. This is a crap task. He wants it done and he wants it dealt. Smouldering is not his idea of 'sorting'. It's dull, dull, dull. It needs poke! And, in his mind, poke means petrol.

He didn't attend many Chemistry lessons, at school. He wasn't considered to be safe in a lab. His teacher always found an early opportunity to send him out. Even when he stayed, he took no notice. Chemistry was a drag - except when an opportunity to light a Bunsen-burner (unbidden) arose. He liked fire. It was forceful.

Slow smouldering is boring. It appears to be almost inactive. It fails either to please or to get the job done. It needs a boost. But, unknown to him, it generates an intense, if unspectacular, heat. Pour petrol on it and it gasps; it inhales. It holds its breath. It shows no instantaneous change. Then, as if the victim of unbearable indigestion, it releases a huge, ripping, echoing fart. It's so violent that it tears its body apart. The noise is incredibly loud. Not just normal loud. It's echoing loud, destructive loud, Hiroshima loud. And whilst, at first, it's all fart and no flame, an elongated pause is followed by a fire-ball. It's so concentrated that it's almost solid. It can floor you. Bruise your ribs; make you breathless; knock you out. And it will set you alight. Clothes, hair, flesh. You will start to melt. And he does.

"Look at my garden, for Christ's sake! Phone the fire brigade!"

"You silly mare! Look at your son. Phone an ambulance!"

All she can see is burning space to be restored. Her son's been dragged into a shower. He's out of it, now. Flame out; focus out. Shivering from a cold drenching but, more so, from shock. That's the killer.

Before he was burned, he'd been banged-up. "Young Offenders' Institution" sounds so much more accommodating than "Prison". Its euphemistic: 'young offender' evokes a being so much softer than 'felon'. And, of course, 'Institution' is a title normally reserved for education and improvement. Jeez, get real!

These guys are bad boys. Some of us may like to find out why they are but let's not kid ourselves: they've done bad things. Bad is what they understand. Bad is the currency of their everyday trade. And bad is what most of them take away with them, come the end of their stint. They've matriculated; they use what they've learned; they're candidates for adult incarceration, come the day.

Our lad is lippy. He likes to dis. To turn a conversation into contradiction. To return complement with contempt. It's what he's learned to do. Parents, siblings, school-mates: sparring partners all. Teachers even more so. They're sparring partners of his own choosing, but opponents, none the less. Had there ever been a period, beyond the cradle, that he had not regarded as being fit for a fight? It's doubtful.

He's playing pool. He's quite handy. There's an undercover bet on and he looks likely to beat his cock o' the rock opponent. That's not supposed to happen. It mustn't happen. Or, if it does happen, there will be consequences. Unpleasant consequences. They've broken the rules, but their rules are stronger than any made by Magistrates, or MPs. Here, there's no room for interpretation, for benefit of the doubt, for once but once, only. Their rules are fixed. Rigid. Unassailable. He may not, must not, win.

But he does. And there's his prize to be claimed. Not drugs – he's done with them. Just fags - but, in here, fags are never 'just'. He lifts his head from the final pot. He replaces his cue it its rack. A mistake, this; he's blowing cooler than makes sense. It's the only cue to be re-racked.

Eyes are engaged. He cannot control his natural urge to mock. His are alive; they lack his opponent's permafrost. His eyes dance and glitter; they display a pleasure in victory, an amusement in defeating the odds, a delight in the prize to be awarded. But there'll be no prize. Prizes are part of the soft world. Here, they're part of the cynicism that informs the way things work. He claims it, nevertheless. And his voice replicates his eyes: it's mocking, triumphant, expectant. He's lippy.

Will the heavy end of the cue that smashes against the left side of his head result in any permanent damage? Will anybody care?

Blues And Twos.

Ambulance first. Then the fire engine. The air filled with sirens and klaxons, strobe-lights pulsing. A stretcher, a hose, men working at speed and with urgency, but no obstructions to the flow of activity. It's like a well-choeographed ballet.

The flames are quenched, leaving nothing more than a greasy film and the stench of sodden ash in the air. A swathed body is lifted aboard the ambulance and, unlike the fire engine's quiet withdrawal, it speeds away, screeching at potential impediments. Next stop: the nearest specialist burns' unit.

He's a mess. Tattered, dripping clothing is quivering in time to his trembling body. He, his sense of what has happened – is happening - is in the way. He needs to be removed from the reality of it. There are things that need to be done that he's best made unaware of. So, a coma is induced. It's for the best. Now, the experts can work on him. First, the clothing needs to be cut away; some of it, being made of man-made fibres, has melted and welded itself to his flesh and some of that flesh is hanging loose, hardly discernible from the material, itself. It's dead. As liable to harbour filth as old-fashioned fly-paper. If shock is the most immediate danger, infection runs it a close second. This body needs to be made clean and to be kept clean, if it's to heal; if it's not going to fall prey to the millions of bacteria that hover over it.

Close-cropped though his hair had been, he's bald now. No eye-brows, nor lashes. His face is not dissimilar to a peeled tomato: red and moistly smooth. Unnatural. It has a pulpy, vulnerable glister to it. The right arm he used to protect his face is the worst-burned of all. Will it grow new flesh or will grafts be needed? They aren't sure, yet. Indeed, at this stage, nothing is certain.

Oddly, the livid scar, running slip-side of his left eye, remains intact, unaffected.

Keeping Shtum.

-

Warning-tap it had most certainly not been. Full-blooded, double-fisted, fore-hand smash, more like. There's a distinctive sound made when a cricket ball catches the meat of a bat. It resonates. You can hear the impact being absorbed by the carefully crafted willow, as it passes through the bat's depth and length. There's nothing tinny-sounding about it; it's rich, deep, almost mellow. And it remains in the air as, far more slowly than you would expect, it gradually fades. Such was the sound made by the assault.

There was no blood. The skin had not broken. But, almost immediately, a livid welt ran from hair-line to cheek-bone. Neither then nor subsequently did it take-on the hues of bruising. It looked more like a birth-mark. It never looked worse, nor did it ever look better.

Bad though these boys were; grim sights though they had witnessed; pain though they were guilty of having inflicted on others, they were stunned. Stunned by the sound of it, by the sight of it; that he was still standing; that he had emitted no cry of pain. Silently, he turned around and, slightly unsteadily, he walked away, made for his cell, and, carefully, he laid down on his bed. Gingerly, he turned onto his left side, crooking his knees, and crossing his clenched fists across his chest.

Around the pool table, there had been no movement and no exchange of any sort.

A warden looks in. To him, it seems as if cock o' the rock has just issued a match challenge and is waiting for his opponent to pick-up a cue before the balls are set-up. He notices an absentee and asks where he is. “Gone for a lie-down.” Then, after a brief pause, “Says he’s got a headache.” The warden nods, turns about, and continues with his free-association- period rounds. He’ll look-in on the lad when he passes by.

But he’s asleep. Or, so it seems. “Best leave him,” the warden reckons.

“You’ll Have To Be Extremely Careful.”

Healing was going to be a slow process. Grafting, it was reckoned, could be avoided. Just. But the tissue was extremely tender, and it would remain tender for years to come. No exposure to intense sunlight. Avoid excessive rises in temperature. Moisturise and keep moisturising. He’s been incredibly, almost unbelievably, lucky; he must not think, “Hey, sorted. No sweat.” Movement will be restricted. Pain will be residual. His face and right arm will be vulnerable to infection way beyond his date of discharge.

And, even all these weeks later, the colour of his face and of his defensive arm is closer to puce than to pink.

The burns’ man had asked no questions about the distinctive scar that the flames had not erased. Not his concern. But, tender as his facial tissue now was, it was an ugly indication of previous violent impact. The warden had asked, when he first saw it. “It’s nothing,” had been the response. “How did you come by it?” had been wasted breath. Persistence would avail nothing;

that much he knew for sure. Nor would any of the others volunteer information. "Arsing around; ran into a door; what a prat, eh?" Was all that was ever said. But it worried him. You don't suddenly acquire a mark like that from arsing around. If it looks that ugly on the surface, what's going-on underneath? Is its colour, its texture anything to do with something way beyond skin-deep? He had no idea - other than he was bloody sure that what he could see should make a doctor stand up and take notice. The boy refused any medical involvement. However, the warden did notice a screwing-up of the left eye that he had been unaware of before. And the boy was periodically sick. By no means all the time. Sometimes, not for ages. Then he would suddenly puke. So without warning was it that it could happen anywhere: during a lesson (he was trying to secure GCSEs in English and Maths); in bed; in the Governor's office. It was considered ill-disciplined behaviour and treated accordingly. He never suggested any alternative explanation.

"What You Need Is A Job!"

It was only a matter of weeks between his release-on-licence and the garden explosion. His Probation Officer had advised that he apply for whatever benefits he was entitled to, so that he was not temptingly short of money. Benefits are neither clear, easily secured, nor immediate in their provision. Meanwhile, the main advantage of being banged-up immediately disappears: bed and board is no longer provided by the State!

The “Big Bang” had been in October. Hospital discharge had come towards the middle of December. As had the first snowfall of winter. He was ‘out of sympathy’ with his parents. And with a sibling who was seeking maximum attention, herself. And with two other siblings whose behaviour did not need a Professor of Psychology to define as being “toxic”. Challenging, this!

Of course, there are sofas to surf and floor-spaces to cadge. There are doorways in which to shelter, over-passes to imitate a roof, skips to snuggle-down in. But this is no way forwards; it’s not even marking-time; sooner or later, there’ll be trouble of one sort or another. Meanwhile, the authorities cite Christmas and New Year as “especially difficult times”. In this, they are not wrong. It’s a thoroughly miserable and disheartening experience. It makes even the stoutest of souls moan and feel sorry for themselves. It prompts the outlook and the question, “Fuck it, why bother?”

“It’s no use whining; what you need is a job and a bit of self-respect!” Unhelpful adult advice, this, indisputable though it may be. But 2 C grade GCSEs, a criminal record, and multiple physical incapacities, due to extensive burns, make for a pretty crap C.V.

“The Trouble Is, You’ve No Experience.”

The Probation Officer can only sympathise. A friend with a social conscience writes to the local M.P. She sympathises and offers to forward the letter to the Justice Minister. A couple of nudges are needed but, eventually, he responds. He sympathises and whilst he can offer no immediate solution, he can offer assurance that the Government is actively involved in addressing this area of concern. It's an on-going issue. Meanwhile, the Government's latest benefits' initiative really is *most* generous. Try it yourself, pal!

To transfer from one system of benefits to another is not a seamless process. You don't retain the one until the necessary paperwork moves you over to the other. You are put on hold. It can take nearly two months. No wage; no benefits. Limbo-land! But, once the new system has settled down, it will be so much better, 'they' say. A disassociated teenager cannot survive for two months, waiting for a bureaucratic system to settle down! Any action that may be taken will smack of one sort of desperation or another.

"So, in an ideal world, what would you like to do to earn a wage?"

"I'm a good driver and I like it."

"Why don't we find a way of getting you a commercial driving licence, then?"

"Banging!"

And so, a short time later, "Well done, you've passed."

"YO!"

It couldn't have been easier, given a willing source of money to pay for the course.

"Ah, I see you had to go away for a while. Sorry, none of our employees has a criminal record."

"The problem is, we like our drivers to have two years' continuous experience. Sorry, mate. Come back when you've got some hours on your tachograph."

"P.T.S.D.? Don't Give Me That!"

We can all understand why USDs and dum-dums, scimitar-wielding fanatics emerging out of and disappearing back into nowhere, mediaeval and public beheadings, way out in the desert, and the like, can make a man less easy-going than once he was. But having your skull stove-in by a mad bastard with a pool cue's no picnic, either. Nor is being lifted off the ground by a home-created H-bomb, only to crash back to earth, aflame.

"You're out, now. Just chill." Chilling don't come cheap. Not money cheap; not time on your hands cheap. How many hours a day can a sane being play X-Box and remain sane? Then there's everyone else out in the lovely sunshine: "Avoid direct sunlight as much as possible," the surgeon had said. Being forced to knock one's head against a brick wall is an acknowledged form of physical torture and humiliation. And it ain't just a Figure of Speech!

"The only way to build-up your hours is job by job; day by day; delivery by delivery." That makes sense. So how to secure these one-off jobs? "This is me; giz a job." "On yer bike, mate,". Or: "Give us a call, later in the week." We all know what that's shorthand for. "I've got a mate who may be able to help you out. Try him on this number." That, too!

Agencies. Of course, they're only really in it, themselves, to earn. We all have to do that. They have no attachment to Social Services, nor Extended Education, nor Work Experience. And, by the time they've taken their cut, or told you the job's been cancelled, or the depot's told you you've been misdirected and need to go elsewhere, or you've been slagged-off for going to the wrong place, as if it's your fault, so the agreed wage is cut, ... it's costing you more to go to work than to stay at home.

"A pride in what you do. A sense of self-reliance. Recognising where you fit into the complex mechanism that forms your workforce. *These* are amongst the reasons for rising of a morning and plying your skills." Thank you, Captain Mainwaring!

Are We Heading For A Happy Ending, Here?

A chanced couple of quid on the lottery raked in a cool million. Of course, it's still not enough to last a life-time. Life-line, however, it most certainly was. It cleared impossible debts. It bought a house, thus eliminating unreasonable rents for unsuitable properties. It bought a bit of time, too. But it does not resolve the contradiction between wanting to work but not being able to on a regular basis because you have no record, yet, of work on a regular basis!

A previously unknown and very distant cousin died, childless, in Australia, leaving thousands of acres of rich pasture land to his only-recorded relative: a youth with a chequered history, back in the old country.

An inspired (and inspiring) entrepreneur, whom he just happened to have met, asked him if he'd like to do simple but vital work with free accommodation thrown-in as part of a generous payment package.

A fabulously wealthy and radical-thinking politician, recognising an ever-deepening social issue, decided it was high-time someone put their money where their mouths were and to set-up a scheme for youngsters who had gone wrong but who wanted to turn their lives around; the scheme was devoted to fast-tracking them into full-time and secure employment.

You reckon? Dream on, mate! This ain't no fairy story. So, what kind of a story is it? What do you honestly think its ending might be? You've got all the facts - and they're what stories are made from: facts. Things that happen to folk. Actually happen. Real folk. Figure it out for yourself; there's a certain inevitability about it, if we're honest. Unless, of course, ... I wonder; you should, too.

The Dunkirk Spirit

May 29th, 2040. A very elderly lady, possessed quite clearly of indomitable spirit and, happily, of good health, stands close to the deck-rails of a cross-channel ferry. There are more comfortable ways of travelling from England to France, especially for one in her centenary year, but she has been adamant: by boat, it must be!

She is accompanied by a man in his late 70s/early 80s, and another, aged around 50. They are joined, subsequently, by a young woman, who must be somewhere in the region of her mid-20s. It is fair to surmise these to be her son, her grandson, and her great-grand-daughter. Certainly, there is both a discernible resemblance in their appearance and a closeness of manner between them to make this more likely than not. Understandably, they are solicitous of her. There has been heavy rain and, whilst it has abated, the decks are slippery. The choppy sea lends their vessel an uncertainty of pitch. Whilst she manages with just one walking stick – and she manages extremely well - they are clearly worried that she may slip, or miss her footing. But she has asked them not to fuss; not to overcrowd her; not to limit the solitary space she so surely needs. As close to the edge of the ferry as she can be; holding onto the safety rail with one hand, her stick suspended from the crook of her arm. In the other hand, she grips a bag. Just an ordinary, supermarket bag, purchased cheaply as a convenient short-term carrier. Quite possibly saved from previous use. She is of a pre-chuck-away generation. The observant amongst her fellow passengers will have noticed that she has not released her grip upon that bag, since boarding.

She looks out across the grey, choppy water, turning her face into the wind, which she allows (even encourages) to stream through her normally neatly-coiffured hair. Her eyes are closed. In prayer? To prevent the wind from making them water? Merely to aid concentration? We can only guess. Since gathering in this particular and exposed area of the ferry, none within the group has said anything. There has been a church service solemnity about them. Eventually, she turns her head and asks, in a firm, clear, distinctive voice: “What time is it?”

“Another three minutes,” the elder man responds. Strictly speaking, it’s not a precise answer to the question asked. It is, however, the answer she was seeking.

“Would you hold the bag, please, darling?” And the young woman steps forward to take the bag from her great-grandmother. Meanwhile, the two men position themselves behind the elderly lady. There is a form of Cenotaph Service precision about this.

The grandson checks his watch. “It’s time,” he announces. As if rehearsed (in all probability, actually rehearsed,) the young woman opens-up the neck of the bag and inclines it towards her great-grandmother, who dips her spare hand into it. She removes a small, neatly-woven wreath. Glossy laurel leaves, tightly bound in a close circle; red berries, equally spaced, and alternated with pure white carnation flower-heads, lend the whole assemblage contrasts in colour and in texture. Firmly affixed to the wreath is a small, white card onto which have been printed three, reduced-size photographs, and there is a hand-written message.

The elderly lady faces out to sea, once again. Her lips move. The words are either silently expressed or so softly spoken that they are lost amidst the noise of the wind. Then, with a steely deliberation surprising from one so elderly, she tosses the wreath, Frisbee-style, into the air. It proves to have sufficient weight about it not to be blowb-back onto the deck. This is an exercise that has been carefully and thoughtfully planned. Whilst it does not travel far, it lingers, momentarily, and then drops into the ferry's wake. The group stands, quietly, heads inconspicuously inclined. Just for a brief while; a minute, at the most. "Right, then," her voice has a benevolent authority about it, "time for coffee - and a tot!" The appendix has a twinkle about it: a relish of naughtiness. "And it's my shout!" She unhooks her stick and releases her grip upon the safety-rail before heading, steadily but with determination, towards the door through which they will be able to regain access to the boat's interior. To its warmth. To its bar and her clearly-stated order: "Four white coffees, please, and four doubles of rum!" The barman invites her and her party to sit at a table, and he will bring the drinks over to them. She thanks him, and they sit; they do not have to wait many minutes before the barman settles the drinks on their table. She lifts her glass into the air and, before she sips its contents, she says, "I never met him, but my mother always talked of how he loved a tot of rum - God bless, him!"

Before it sinks, let's catch a glimpse of the still-floating wreath. More particularly, of its white card attachment. A photograph of a young woman; the hairstyle dates the image pretty accurately. Another photograph; this one is of a young man. Early twenties; a cheeky grin; army uniform. And, one final photo. A baby, just a few months old, looking much like any other baby. Swaddled, as was the way, then; a gummy smile. The already-running ink bears a single, factual message: "*100 years ago, this day. 29.v.40.*"

With A Nod To Geoffrey C.

The Electricians' Tale.

On Mary's Bridge, in Derwent-cradling Derbie, our scene is set. That ancient Roman camp-site, where legions rested from their northwards march to re-enforce the stony structure of Hadrian's design. A house, still standing, many centuries after its foundation.

Early-laid bricks, supported by herring-bone-slanting timbers may, even now, be seen, six centuries after they were hammered into place. Tudor folk expanded it, as did Georgians, too. Then there came Victorians: inventors and innovators, all. Much change and many strange occurrences has this habitation seen, since first it stood: The Bridge House of St. Mary.

But none so strange as once, come Hallow E'en, just after electricity was installed.

Its owners, then, were merchant burghers, made rich by silk, and quite determined to reveal what wonders their accumulated wealth could purchase. Wax-bespattered flambeaux and gas-scorched sconces were replaced by wall-mounted lanterns, casting within the house's many rooms a brilliance never seen since first those walls were raised. And that, as we now know, was centuries before this tale, which now I tell.

But of these burghers, first, I needs must mention. At his table's head sat Obadiah Smith, descended from a line of men whose livelihoods had rested in their skilful hands. Obadiah was the eldest son of Jethro, who in his turn had Festus for a sire. Smiths were they all, i'faith.

The good lady wife of Obadiah was Felicia named and she had been the only infancy-surviving child of siblings five. This worthy couple's pride and joy, the daughter they so doted on, was Hermione-Rose. Their only child. A girl whose peach-perfect complexion was framed by self-curling tresses spun from strands of gilded auburn. Her eighteen years had offered undiluted pleasure to her mama and her papa.

Into their closely self-contained existence (cooks, maids, beneath-stairs valets and outdoor ostlers, besides,) stepped Victor (named in honour of his Queen-Empress) and his strapping son, Albert, (in honour of her Consort Prince): purveyors of electrical marvels, both.

Lengths of wiring, neatly plaited, brought this twain into the house and with them fixtures meet to furnish palaces grander by far than our modest, Derwent-over-arching house on Mary's Bridge. And with good cheer did Victor and his sturdy son, the youthful Albert, set about their work. Accomplished whistlers were they both and, as they went about their daily tasks, they filled the house with music.

Love them dearly though she did, Hermione-Rose found her parents to be dutiful but dull. 'Propriety' was their watch-word in everything they did. And propriety practised from cock-crow-to-curfew, each day of her eighteen living years, had taken its due toll. Not that she was consciously aware of this. Not, that is, until the ever-obliging Victor and, more especially, the broad-beaming-and-shouldered Albert alerted her more clearly. Not by premeditated representation but, rather, unknowingly, as they brought light, life, and laughter to even the most menial of tasks, like feeding flex into walls of cavity. This was, she hoped, labour that long would last.

Now Albert, it transpired, was within a day or twain of equal age with Hermione-Rose. But his life's embrace had been as different from her own as life's embrace could offer. His mother, Victor's missis, loved a laugh - almost as much as she loved a steaming pot of tea; or, indeed, a glass or two of stout.

On Fridays, after supper, she and Victor would "make an evening of it", as she used to say. This, as regularly as others might attend an early-morning-mass. When he was younger, Albert and his siblings would also tag along. To a nearby Public House, or a Music Hall turn, or the extravaganza of a Travelling Circus; sometimes there were dances held in the Recruiting Sergeant's Drill Hall; at other times, an impromptu sing-along would be the object of their once-weekly pleasure. Albert had loved them all, and relished every moment. Such was a world unknown to, let alone by, Hermione-Rose. It was a world that had taught him to whistle.

Room by room, candle light and gas jets were replaced by an at-the-flick-of-a-switch source of a fresh effulgence. Victor and Albert, it seemed, were latter-day sorcerers. They had embraced the miraculous. Embraced it; harnessed it; delivered it to the lost-in-wonderment family, Smith. The most lost and the greatest in wonderment: Hermione-Rose.

And so there came along a Hallow E'en; the eighteenth of her sheltered life, thus far.

Dark, it was, and cold, with a star-encrusted sky. It was the night of restless souls. Prelude to the morrow's symphony of sainthood. A night to lock doors and to bar windows. To stoke bright fires and, if you were extremely lucky (as were the Smiths) to enjoy the securing brilliance offered by electricity.

And then it began to falter, to flicker, this recent installation. After flickering came failure.

Mr Smith, who understood about value for money and how you should get what you have paid for, summoned Victor. But it was young Albert who arrived, a little while later. It was a Friday. Victor and his missis were "making an evening of it." Hermione-Rose, who had of late harboured certain doubts generated by Messers Darwin, Spencer, and their following, felt her faith in the power of prayer refreshed.

During the period of installation, the pretty and trained-to-be-pure-in-mind-and-spirit Hermione-Rose had taken notice much closer by far than was assumed to be appropriate either to her status or to her gender. Her fluttering heart had found itself a rival of her fast-learning mind. She now knew how to set the house lights a-flickering and a-failing. And, of course, she was quite determined that her recently acquired education should not have ended, yet. Albert had shown himself so willing to share his wisdom, thus far. She felt sure that his resources were yet nowhere near exhausted.

"Papa," said she, "Mama," and she let her eye-lids lower, as her under-lip protruded. "I fear that our meddling with Nature sits ill with this night's other forces. Retire, I shall, and devote myself to slumber, till haply will the morrow dawn with all its Saints, triumphant!"

So blessed, these parents. So undeserving of such a daughter dear.

And thus, with their consent and blessing, did Hermione-Rose repair unto her room. Where, - would you have ever guessed it? - young Albert was preparing to apply the accumulated knowledge of his eighteen years.

The morrow dawned. Much intermittent and electric flickering, overnight, had given way to a regular and steady output. The master of the house exhibited much concern that Albert's duties should have lasted through hours so long. No bill presented would be too steep and cash (the master would hear no argument against) was to be paid. To Obadiah and to his fond Felicia, there was no cost too great that could re-pay the young man's long night's loss of sleep and his restoration of electric light that had brought such blithe suffusion to their darling daughter's cheeks!

THE BATTLE OF MALDON

{An experiment in transposing Anglo-Saxon alliterative & narrative verse into modern prose.}

... The rain ran in runnels down the soldiers' faces. The trees wept tears, sensitive, perhaps, to the turmoil that lay ahead. Byrhtnoth, the brave commander, ordered Offa's kinsman to dismount and to move forwards on foot. Recognising his leader's determination to endure neither failure nor fear, the kinsman released his favourite falcon, leaving it to fly freely through the forest. A sure sign that he was willing to lose his life at Byrhtnoth's bidding. Eadric dismounted, too, shaking his spear and brandishing his broadsword, in a style that asserted his determination to destroy his master's foes.

Byrhtnoth began to boost his soldiers' appetite for battle. He checked their equipment, roused their spirits, and ensured that each wielded their weapons in their most effective manner. Once he was certain that all was set, he, too, dismounted and joined his best-trained troops.

Their rendezvous was the river. On the opposing side of the flooded ford stood a burly Viking envoy. He bellowed his sailors' blunt instruction: "Pay or repent!" He went on to tell the Saxons that they were better to surrender gold than guts. He balanced this belligerence with false fairness, promising that simple payment would ensure his navy's swift return to Norse seas.

Byrhtnoth would brook neither bullying nor blandishments. He shook his shield and slashed at the air with his spear. His blood was boiling, and his determination not to be subdued shaped his speech: "Listen to these, my lingering last words on this, your shoddy pursuit of pernicious larceny. Neither I, nor my force, will fall to your feeble threats and tedious attempts to persuade us to fail in our duty to protect the land and laws of Aethelred, our rightful ruler. Retreat or regret it! Should you choose to fight, we shall flay you and flail you, hack you and hew you, stab you and slay you. We will not pay one penny to appease your vile invasion of our shores. Return this reply to your pirate-patron!"

The tidal river was in full flood and it would be hours until its flow abated. From bank to bank they cursed and chaffed each other, firing insults and flinging goads. Bloody banter, jagged japes, and foul-mouthed filth was catapulted across the broiling brine of Blackwater River.

At last, the tide turned. The ford now offered access to both invaders and defenders alike. A malevolent Viking took first stand on his side; Byrthnoth ordered Wulfstan, a battle-hardened veteran, to stand opposed. This son of the courageous Ceola stepped-up and, in full fury, let fly his spear which felled the foremost Viking invader. Immediately, Wulfstan was joined by Aefere and Maccus, another pair of pure-bred battlers. This trio parried any spears and arrows projected against them. The invaders recognised that they were hemmed-in; any victory would require great violence and result in a monstrous mountain of mortality. More room to move was needed. They proffered a pause and asked for time to re-deploy.

Bravely, but boastfully, Byrthnoth gave ground. In spirit, glorious, but, in strategy, too generous? He then called upon his counterpart to let the clash commence, truthfully failing to foresee to which side victory may avail. The river was now shallow, and its bed may be invaded. Both sides deployed their battle lines, Byrhtnoth central amidst his countrymen. Suddenly, a frenzy of ferocity unfolded. Ear-splitting noise echoed all around; it was as if the earth had erupted. Spears, short and long, flew through the air, arrows found their targets, shields defended, clashed, and clouted. It was a furious affair and many men lay dead or wounded. Byrhtnoth's nephew, Wulfmaer, perished; Prince Eadwaerd vowed vengeance and succeeded in slicing through a Viking's side with his broadsword. On and on the battle raged: demented, destructive, deadly. Aristocrat fought commoner, the young paid no regard to age, regulations were disregarded. It was slaughter or be slaughtered.

Byrhtnoth, himself, suffered a spear wound; he smashed the shaft with his shield, leaving the head buried in his bowel. Enraged, he gained revenge, pushing a spear deep into his assailant's throat-protector, followed by a second which split it and, thus, with a twist, was driven home. His foe folded and fell. One of Aethelred's personal servants suffered a wound; a boy came to his aid. Wulmaer, who was Wulfstan's son, was a lad, a mere child, but he was decisive, too. Mortal though the wound may be, he grabbed the grievous spear and tore it out, turning in one movement and returning it with well-timed might, thus finishing-off the once-defiant foeman. Another Viking, more concerned to corner Byrhtnoth and to steal his gems than to engage in fair fight, advanced upon him; the elderly Earl spotted him and sought to defend himself. He took hold of his well-wrought sword, slicing through his attacker's tunic, but, out of his sight, another Viking intervened, knocking that gilt-handled weapon from his hand. For him, it was the end. With his dying breath he rallied his troops and, stooping to kneel, he said his prayerful penitence, seeking solace for his sorrows and salvation for his soul. Having regained their breath, his attackers hacked at him, dealing death blows, at last, and dispatching Aelftnoth and Wulmaer, who had rushed to his defence, with equal lust and loathing.

Panic persisted. Odda's sons scattered. Godric, who had been gifted by his leader mounts a plenty over the years, fled the field of battle. And, worse still, on Byrhtnoth's own horse, too. His brothers, Godrinc and Godwig, were close behind him. They were not alone. As Offa, himself, had once predicted: kind gifts granted are swiftly forgotten; claimed courage easily turns to cowardice, when put to the test.

Even so, fewer fled than defended with fortitude. Urged forwards by Aelfric's inspirational young son, and by Aelfwine's words, counter-defence became counter-attack. "Think how it will be," he said, "when all is over. When, as we drink together having survived, and we exchange stories. Who will be noted for courage and who for cant? Whose tales will ring true and whose fall flat? Which of you will be marked 'brave' and which of you 'boastful'? I mean to prove my worth; I'm of noble Mercian stock and nobility is my nature." And, with that, he flung himself back into battle.

Offa, as he readied himself for a return to arms, responded with these words: "Aelfwine has set the target. Those of us left must fight or die; we must do so in our dead leader's name and restore his reputation for, by fleeing on Byrhtnoth's horse, Godric has tricked some into believing that they have been misled and that he who now lies dead forsook them by fleeing the field. This has brought division and dissent."

In this, he received support from Leofsunu, who vowed never to flee nor to surrender. Come what may, his own people would never be able to claim him to be a coward. He, too, re-armed and re-engaged. Dunnere, a lowly not a lordly man, followed suit. And so did a hostage named Aescferth. Eadweard the Long vowed he would not give an inch of ground and his vow was validated when, having pierced the Danish redoubt, he perished beneath a barrage of blows. His example was followed. Sibyrht's brother, Aetheric, charged and barged his way into the enemy's midst, maiming as he moved; Offa ousted an enemy; but, alas, both were slaughtered, fitting fighters for their generous liege-lords. Gadd's kinsman was killed, too, along with Wigelm's son. Meanwhile, Thurstan's son, Wistan, threw himself into the fray. It was a fearsome sight. Combatants clawed their way over corpses; blackened blood besmirched the smudged-green margins of the river; there was clashing, and gnashing, and thrashing; howls and wails filled the air, itself defiled by the sickening stench of death.

No matter what, as some leaders fell others filled their roles. The brothers Oswold and Ealdwald, joined by the aged Byrthwold, rallied their followers, urging them never to despair, never to surrender. The old man's voice quivered, as he shook his spear, "May our hearts be sounder, our spirits be surer, our intent be fiercer, as we fall and grow fewer! Though I am old, I shall not falter. My lord lies low; I care not whether I live-on or lose my life. I shall never relinquish my loyalty."

Wonderful words: proud, if not prudent; pure, patriotic, and perfect. They prompted Aethelgar's son, Godric (not the one who fled) to re-engage in battle. He hacked his way to the heart of the conflict, killing and creating chaos as he scurried and scrummaged, brandished and burrowed, clashed and collided. Caught, at the last, by the cut that cost him his life. ...

{What remains of this ancient poem, thought to have been composed not long after the actual, historical battle it describes, and which was fought in 991, is an incomplete fragment and, as such, lacks both its opening and its closing lines. That we have the fragment, at all, is a miracle: the only known surviving manuscript was destroyed during a fire in 1731; however, a transcript of that manuscript had been made, which was discovered, subsequently.)

Rob Worrall read English at The University of Kent, and then spent the next 35 years teaching it to teenagers.

Now retired, he divides his time between 'extreme gardening' and 'scribbling': short stories, an on-line reading diary, and theatre revues of performances at Nottingham Playhouse for an internet magazine.

He has absolutely no plans to join others in pursuit of sinking a small, white ball into a series of slightly larger holes, prior to seeking solace in the nineteenth of them!

Printed in Great Britain
by Amazon